LADDER OF ANGELS

BRIAN THOMPSON

Slow Dancer Press

Published in Great Britain in 1999 by
Slow Dancer Press
91 Yerbury Road London N19 4RW

British Library Cataloguing-in-Publication Data.
A catalogue record for this book is available from the British
Library.

ISBN 1 871033 48 9

Slow Dancer Fiction titles are available in the U.K. through
Turnaround Publisher Services and in the U.S.A. through Dufour
Editions inc.

———————————————

Cover design: Keenan

Printed in Great Britain by The Guernsey Press Co. Ltd.

This book is set in Sabon 10/13

Slow Dancer Press

LADDER OF ANGELS

Slow Dancer Press

Pour Paulette Ayraud

ONE

Mrs Evans was teaching me the tango. As it happened, I already knew the rudiments of this exciting dance, but never as interpreted by Mrs Evans, naked save for her high heels and some Mexican silver earrings – a present, she claimed, from Acapulco. The high heels were there to add grace and I suppose authenticity, but even with them on, the lady's head barely reached my chin. We swooped about the room, exceedingly drunk, to the most famous tango of them all, the Blue one. It was past two in the morning and the rain that had been forecast had arrived as grounded cloud, moping blindly about the streets, tearful and incoherent. But we were okay – we were up on the third floor, looking down on the damn cloud and having a whale of a time. Mrs Evans was warm and moist to the touch and her make-up was beginning to melt. For some reason a piece of Sellotape was stuck to her quivering bottom, and as we danced I tried to solve this small but endearing mystery. It came to me at last: it was her sister's birthday and earlier in the evening she had parcelled up a head scarf, some knickers and a Joanna Trollope paperback.

"To hell with it," she cried at last, pushing me into an armchair and jumping up onto my lap like a child, her arms round my neck. I cuddled her with real affection. She was in many ways the perfect landlady.

"I was a fool to take you in, Mr Patrick Godalmighty Ganley, and I'm an even bigger fool to chuck you out," she panted.

"I shall be very sorry to go."

"The pint-sized Mrs Evans. And not bad for a mother of two. Now what's all this bullshit about a job?"

"An exacting commission. I have been commissioned by clients I am not at liberty to name."

"My God! They must be absolutely bloody desperate."

"That, or bent as a butcher's hook, yes."

I could just reach my whiskey and water with my free hand. I sipped and passed her the glass. There were unexpected tears in her eyes. We kissed. The room, like her whole life, depended upon chaotic friendliness for its effects. Gujerati cushions and pillows were heaped up against one wall. There were three massive floor lamps fashioned from acid carboys filled with coloured marbles. Most of the furniture, like Mrs Evans herself, was very low to the ground.

"Say you'll miss me, you bastard."

I kissed her plump little shoulder.

"Life won't be the same."

"I shall miss you," she said at last, her head buried now against my faithless heart. Grey tiptoed from her roots.

She was really called Tania, and she ran a little ethnic boutique in a prime position on the pedestrian precinct, opposite Woolworths. We were in the North of England, of course – anywhere south of the Trent she would have been stoned in the streets as a fatuous, pathetic under-achiever. Up here, she

8

was what she was – merry and bright, sardonic, gifted. The Gujerati cushions and the Mexican earrings came from stock in the shop, which also sold Japanese crockery, African bead jewellery and the like. Before opening a business and in the days of her youth, she had been a very good painter. That was in the period when you could go out and buy a few tins of house paint from a very different kind of Woolworths and do your thing on a sheet of eight by four. She had kept some of these student paintings and some she had sold. The ones she kept were of figures and showed a woman – herself – luxuriating on a bed while a wan parent sat looking out of the window, anywhere, in order not to be associated with all this pale and unambiguous nakedness.

There was a Mr Evans. Once he had been her tutor. He had a sixties' head of hair, and teeth stained brown from smoking: he also lived in the town, but under more obscure circumstances. Alan taught at the Pre-Dip college and made occasional huge aluminium sculptures. They were the sort of thing you see in small German towns outside the Rathaus, often with yellow water trickling mournfully over their planes. There was not much call for them in this country, however. Alan Evans consoled himself with a bit of teaching, drinking each lunchtime at the Cherry Tree, and screwing a gloriously healthy student of his called Gail. He talked through his nose, rolled his own, and was, in the undemanding ambience of the arts in Yorkshire, total bon ton. His bible was Camus' *The Myth of Sisyphus*. His other reading comprised comics.

Tania Evans was the mother of two boys by this good-natured and indolent man. One busked the alto sax for a living, the other was doing Business Studies. We were all pals together – the boys, their parents, Gail and I. It went further still – to like Tania, you also had to like her rather soppy friends Sandy and Pip. To like Alan and Gail, you had to take on board Gail's mum and dad, her brother Rick and his girl Shazza. This entire tribe of people met amicably every Sunday without fail at the Volunteer. It was a free house, but we only ever drank Tetley's. Gail's mum thought it was all a bit iffy, but everyone else seemed to think it was just great. We supped some stuff out at the Vollie, we did that.

"Christmas soon upon us," Gail's dad said, managing to make it just his humble opinion.

"Soon comes round, Frank."

We were widdling away the fourth pint in the fragrant little shack at the back of the pub.

"Tania says you're off, then?"

"You have it to do."

"Aye, you do that. They say you've been dancing bloody tango until all hours."

"That's it."

He buttoned himself up slowly and carefully and ran his hands under the icy tap.

"Work is it, that calls you away?"

"Something like that."

He nodded. He was a bit of a jewel, Gail's old dad. Next day, he walked to the station and caught the train to Hertford. Via Leeds, change at Stevenage.

The contrast with Yorkshire was stark. A terrible death of the spirit had evidently overtaken this part of the kingdom. Walking into town from the station you had the feeling that the last person alive with sentiment and intelligence, with some glimmering of hope for the future had, a few weeks ago, cried *fuck it* and joined the queues at the video libraries. They were driving up to the damn video shops at six in the evening in their fuel-injected Cavaliers and coming out with armfuls of horror. The living dead were catching up on news of their friends and relatives. They were tossing thirty or forty million dollars worth of production into the back seat and taking off for home and hell.

And was there no one to reprehend all this? Indeed there was. Mr Anthony Pelling owned a tall Edwardian house on a hill near the County Library. He himself was tall and thin, like the house, and gave off a faintly antique whiff. His eyes swam like naked oysters behind fogey specs and his adam's apple could cut breeze blocks. He received me in a knocked through drawing room furnished with elaborate care. It was one of those places where every table has a telling little display of shells and Victorian spectacle cases, or quaint old Mummetshire button moulds. It was not the house of smokers, or drinkers of bottled beer. Pelling moved cautiously as if in fear of stumbling or going ape suddenly and breaking something priceless. Without asking for it I was given an appalling glass of French polish, passed off as amontillado. My host sipped his sherry thoughtfully, gazing the while at my trainers.

"Is the North your home?" he asked.

"I was born in Lambeth. Like William Blake."

"Oh yes," he muttered, "Blake. And so, um, what were you doing in the North?"

"You wouldn't want me to break a rule of confidentiality," I said, thinking of Tania and her bacon sandwiches. "I was working on a case, naturally. I think you have my most recent references."

These had been prepared most fulsomely to my dictation by Gail and her brother Rick, who was a word-processor buff. Pelling nodded. The frown was still obstinately glued to his face. A marmalade cat was studying us on the wrong side of the double glazing. Its mouth opened and shut in pink silence. Master lit a brass swan neck lamp and studied the effect, as if he had just done something pretty outrageous. He walked to

11

the window and drew the curtain on the astonished cat. Then he sat down opposite me and we each pursued our private thoughts. Much did I care. I had already stuck him for the train fare.

"I would like you to find my daughter," Pelling said at last.

"So you say in your letter. Do you mean find her, or make some effort to find her?"

"I don't quite follow."

"Presumably you've already tried all the obvious things – police, the Salvation Army, other charities. Failing to find her within a certain time span is going to be no problem at all. Actually finding her might take time and money."

"How much are we talking?" he asked with the first sign of common sense.

"Thirty a day, the hire of a car, a minimum of a hundred a week in itemised expenses. If she's abroad, we start again."

"This is not a little expensive!"

"I'm trying to tell you – I can spend enough of your money to salve your conscience, or I can find her. It's up to you."

After drumming for a while with his brittle nails, he withdrew a photograph from the drawer of a sofa table. I had expected his daughter to be in her late twenties. The photograph showed a girl of sixteen or so. Pelling was watching me closely to see whether I would break out in a wild yahoo.

"This is Melissa," he said.

In the picture, Melissa was wearing a knee-length nylon toga and a cardboard Roman helmet. She held up a wooden short sword by the arm that carried her wristwatch and there was a further anachronistic touch provided by her Clem Atlee glasses. All in all, she seemed a defensive sort of kid. I swallowed painfully. Pelling goggled at me with a father's quiet pride.

"This is recent?"

"It was taken two years ago."

"She didn't leave home dressed like this?"

"Are you being facetious?"

"These are all routine questions."

He took back the print, and in a curious gesture, wiped down the emulsion with his handkerchief.

"This is the only photograph we have of her."

"I shall need to copy it. Is your wife at home?"

"My wife and I are separated," Pelling said, after a pause.

"But you've spoken to her. About your daughter."

"Yes, of course."

"And?"

He glanced at his watch. I had already sent him a questionnaire, which he passed over in a buff envelope. The telephone rang and was answered immediately in another room. Pelling took my glass away from me.

"I have to go out to dinner in a few moments. That is, I am driving to Cambridge. Is there anything else you need?"

"I should like to see her room."

She lived at the top of the house in a large dormer room. As we ascended, the comforts of the house diminished. Melissa's bed was cold and cheerless. A pine chest of drawers was supported under one leg by the *Stanley Gibbons Omnibus* for 1956. Teddy sat with his legs apart, looking bored and truculent. The back of his head rested against a poster of the Kings and Queens of England. Pelling Sahib had pots of money, his daughter pots of pencils and ridiculously thin water colour brushes.

"Is your daughter artistic?"

"Most children are," Dad muttered.

She had one of those drop-leaf school bureaus with tricky little drawers and partitions. They contained a few dusty paper clips and rubber bands. Her bottle of Quink was

13

prominent. Her essays on Bismarck and Disraeli were neatly filed. A marked copy of *Julius Caesar* partially explained the cardboard Roman helmet.

"Is Melissa your only child?"

"Yes, of course," Pelling said.

"Would you say she was quiet, diligent? Did she have what you might call the Roman virtues?"

His glasses flashed angrily.

There were no surprises in her chest of drawers. All her underwear was white cotton. Her blouses were beautifully ironed and folded. She did not appear to own any clothes whatsoever bearing a legend or logo, surely some kind of record. She was a generous 34C cup and size 14. She had a swimsuit, but it was sheathed in a plastic bag from the National Trust. The colour was apple green. There were no letters, or postcards from friends. No photographs, souvenirs or knick-knacks. The evidence of her bedroom suggested a big girl with large chunks of her brain missing.

"It's a filthy job you do," Pelling muttered in disgust.

I glanced at him with curiosity.

"I shall need to talk to your wife."

"As you wish."

"Who answered the phone a moment ago?"

"My housekeeper," he said, glancing at his watch.

The second and third attic bedrooms were stored with furniture. There was a little cupboard at the head of the stairs. It contained her hockey stick and a Droopy and Brown bag. Inside that were stuffed tights, knickers and bras.

"For the needy children of the world," I suggested.

But Pelling was already heading back downstairs.

Pilar – the housekeeper – was even more of a shock than Melissa's Roman helmet. She was about twenty-five and must have been a constant source of fascination to the neighbours. Loony Pelling elbows his wife and gains a Philippine wench of startling eroticism. Little and lithe, she wore a button through dress and cork heeled sandals. Her thin wrist supported an amber bead bracelet. The most delicate of gold chains hid in the hollows of her collarbones. It was true she wore rather daft red-framed specs, but these she took off to talk to me. She nibbled on the ear pieces with tiny teeth.

"Melissa was such a hard-working girl," she said. "I have told Anthony she works too hard, is too serious. Not that she should be flippant or anything. But she is unusual for this day and age."

"My impression too," I said. Pilar looked at me without the light of friendship in her eyes.

"I admire private people. Mr Pelling is quite private. I don't find this a fault."

"Did you talk often to the child?"

"We chatted about things on the news, or what there was in the papers. We would talk in this way, yes. She liked to watch me cook. She asked questions about South East Asia, that sort of thing."

"Girl talk," I suggested with plonking irony. "How long have you worked for Mr Pelling?"

"Since his wife left – about a year. A year next month, in fact."

"And before that? What did you do before that?"

She hesitated. Maybe she wanted to tell me she was a senior stewardess on Quantas or a top model or something. We struggled in silence together. The kitchen clock ticked.

"I was a hotel receptionist. In London, of course."

"Miss the rough and tumble?"

"You are unpleasantly conceited," Pilar murmured. She put on her glasses to indicate that the interview was drawing

15

to a close. All the underwear in the top floor cupboard next to the kid's hockey stick was her's and I wanted to ask her about that. She was a silk and little pink bows person It was interesting.

"I really have lots to do," she said.

"Okay. But – just for laughs – where do *you* think the girl is?"

And she did laugh, but more from pity than anything else.

"Oh dear. Is that how its done? It seems very ... what's the word...?"

"Obvious," I said.

I walked down the hill and found an underpass across the four lane highway that had so negligently swept Hertford to one side some time in the sixties. There were graffiti painted and sprayed as far as an arm could reach and a faint ammoniac stench. I walked slowly down the concrete tunnel, hearing the traffic boom overhead. It was that season of the year when even the strongest light bulb seems as yellow as butter. I was feeling tetchy.

Hertford used to be a fine old town of wheat and barley farmers. Four rivers here converge and the Normans liked the look of the place. Today it has all the character of an empty burger box, with which its streets are liberally strewn. I walked into the first pub I came to and ordered a pint, trying to imagine Melissa walking home through these same sorry streets, her head full of Julius Caesar, the welcome of a single bar electric fire up in the attic and Teddy for company. I liked her for leaving. She had a choice of two British Rail stations and a bus terminus.

After pulling the pint, the barmaid went back to her stool and lay with her head on her arms. She was only doing her job. Nobody lived in Hertford any more. They simply came home to sleep. That was its contemporary beauty, not the castle, nor

16

the excellent beer still brewed in the town, but its position on a travel map out of London. That's what the town had become now – Outer London. The first circle of hell.

On the wall of the underpass a few yards from where I sat somebody had written in thick custardy paint *Melissa is a slag*. I could round up all the Melissas in this town of Melissas, Annabels, Damians and Grants, and begin a slow process of elimination. But that was not the point. The point, it seemed to me, was neither her parents nor the svelte Pilar had seen this daub. Or if they had, had walked past with lips like zippers.

"Wake up," I called gently to the girl behind the bar.

"Same again?"

"No, just wake up. You're a long time dead."

TWO

It was easy to see why Diane Pelling had fallen out of favour with her husband, and he with her. They were not on the same page at all. She opened the door of Goose Cottage in an RAF greatcoat that presumably did service as her dressing gown, for under it there was a cotton nightie that was torn at the front. Her broad feet were bare. None of the careful Pelling dispositions here – none of the collectible junk scattered about. In Goose Cottage, Johnny Mathis was on the turntable, yesterday's toast under the grill. One really good painting hung slightly askew on the sitting room wall. At least twenty empty wine bottles were playing sentries on the kitchen floor. Pots in the sink, Scharma's *Citizens* on the draining board, together with a dozen dead matches and the peel from two or three oranges.

The unbuttoned epaulettes to Mrs Pelling's dressing gown wiggled like bunny ears as she received my introduction. I said I thought I might have called at an inconvenient time; to which she gently pushed past me and peered out myopically at the rain.

"Is it still bucketing down? It can't be. Do you think the river will rise high enough to flood this dump?"

"Not for an hour at least."

"Terrific. You couldn't be an angel and light the fire, make some coffee while I have a bath?"

"Nothing simpler."

She paused before retreating, a warm good-natured woman straight from bed.

"There's someone upstairs," she murmured. "A friend."

"Would he like coffee?"

"No. He's leaving."

The little cottage had once overlooked a perfect Corot landscape. Poplars swayed ecstatically on the horizon. I took off her Johnny Mathis and found Radio 3 on the tuner. Brahms. Fine by me. Fine by her too it would seem, for although the white baby grand jammed into one corner of the room doubled as table, plant stand, bottle bank and coat rack, some Schumann was propped up on the music stand. The room was a different sort of chaos from the one I had grown used to in Yorkshire – altogether more hapless. One way or another, either by choice or a long catalogue of failures, Diane Pelling had accepted in herself that she was not a very house person at all.

While I was emptying the grate of a week's wood ash, a young lad who might have been a builder came downstairs, nodded to me, and left. Though the month was November and for all I knew the end of the world had been announced on breakfast television, so dark and dreary was it outside, he wore only a T-shirt on his upper half. I watched him get into the pick-up that was parked outside and drive away on side lights. I made a fire, emptied the ashtrays, straightened the cushions, lit the lamps.

She was someone who read *The Independent*, belonged to the Arts Guild, stayed at home a lot and liked to drink. She had probably built the bookshelves herself – they were made

19

from melamine planks supported on house bricks. Bills and letters were tucked between the books, as well as a biscuit tin of sewing materials, an alarm clock on its back, and many wallets of photographs. Back copies of magazines and newspapers, unopened mail shots and paperbacks lay in cascades at the side of her battered chair. She was knitting someone – herself? – a tam o'shanter.

The sound of her sliding and squeaking about in the bath upstairs made a pleasant backdrop to these investigations. I washed up her pots and threw away the old toast. In the pedal bin a used condom sat on a nest of potato peelings. Her taste in coffee was expensive – and there was enough garlic scattered about in that kitchen to fend off the gloomy Count forever. Stuck to the side wall of the fridge was a Robert Mapplethorpe postcard and a view of Barcelona. I was finding much to like in her.

When she came down she was wearing jeans and a pale pink sweatshirt, her head turbanned by a towel. I noticed that she continued with her wedding ring. Without make-up, her expression was distressingly vacant and absent-minded. She rummaged around in the cushions of the couch for her glasses, and when she put them on, suddenly became beautiful. I passed her the coffee and she parted her lips in a faint smile.

"What do you know about children?" she asked without preamble.

"Do you mean do I have any?"

"You don't," she said. "Anyone can tell that. I don't know too much, and Tony even less."

"Your daughter is eighteen now, is that right?"

"Nearly nineteen."

She had that knack of looking you straight in the eye, but searchingly. She was looking for friends, compadres. As to physical presence, she was comfortably and insouciantly plump. She unwound her turban and combed out her hair with her fingers. She cocked her head endearingly: my turn to speak.

"I have to ask you: do you have any reason to suppose Melissa is in danger? Or could come to harm from anyone?"

"From whom? Of course not. Melissa is careful, cautious. She's a bit of an owl, actually, but I don't think for a moment she's in any physical danger, no. She doesn't like me much and I can't hold that against her. But it does mean that I'm just about the last person she'd ever confide in. Nevertheless."

"You can't see what all the fuss is about?"

"I didn't say that, smart arse."

She asked me for a cigarette with the casualness of a real smoker. I felt – for the first time, I felt – intrusive. Diane Pelling smiled again. I put her at about forty-two, forty-three.

"Go on, then, ask me another."

"How about problems?"

"Name some."

"Money."

She looked perplexed. The Pellings obviously had no problems with silly old money. I tried another tack.

"How about the new housekeeper?"

"That whore? Even with her rouging her nipples in the bathroom we're still just about the most boring family in the Home Counties."

"Maybe she left because she was bored, then."

"That's why *I* did," Mum said calmly.

I could imagine Pelling grinding his teeth to twenty years of such stuff. Diane made an effort to dry her hair by kneeling on all fours in front of the fire. Her bum was not inconsiderable. The soles of her feet were already black from the unswept carpets.

"How long have you lived here?"

21

"It was his mother's. We kept it on after she died. I bought it from him a year ago. Well, I didn't actually buy it. I signed an agreement to purchase or get out."

"Did Melissa get on with Granny?"

"You are joking," Diane said fervently. "Why do you think Granny was packed off out here? That bloody woman was poison."

"How about your folks?"

"She liked them. They're both dead."

"Are there aunts, uncles?"

"No," she said after the slightest of hesitations.

She sat back and dragged vigorously at her scalp. Lucky woman, the curls just bounced out. She picked up her coffee mug and held it in both palms. She grinned.

"This is nice," she said. "But shouldn't you have a trench coat or something, like Bob Mitchum?"

"At the cleaners. Did you and your husband row in front of her?"

"You couldn't row with Tony. It would be like arguing with a stick insect. Do you mean was she peeping through keyholes watching me being beaten up by him? No."

"How about getting screwed by the gardener?"

She jumped suddenly, laughing.

"I feel in the mood to hoover. Would you mind? I don't often get the urge and it won't take a minute."

So, while she trundled about, singing and cursing, I went upstairs for a pee. The bathroom was littered with towels, newspapers, paperbacks. It smelt of pine salts. I took a look in the bedroom. The bed was rumpled and her clothes strewn about. A coffee-coloured bra hung whimsically from the handlebars of her exercise bike. Her bedside reading was a biography of Flaubert. She was on pp 87-88. It was all very appealing. There could be many worse ways of whiling away the hours than by sitting in bed with Diane Pelling, watching the glint of the sky-reflecting water meadows and waiting for the river to burst its banks. I even liked her duvet.

When I came down there were two large gin and tonics on the coffee table. Beside them was a Boots photographic wallet. It explained why Melissa's dad was so short of snapshots. His wife had them all. The most recent showed a very different girl to the Roman centurion. She lay on her back in Majorca sunshine, her plump but solid looking flesh covered here and there by a skimpy brown bikini. In the same sequence – on the same holiday – was a shot of her sitting in a disco or club, wearing a baby blue T-shirt and terrific white beach trousers. Diane sat beside her looking her years and wearing a little Monsoon number.

"She takes after you," I said gallantly.

"I should hope so. She's nothing like me in personality, of course. And by the way, the boy who was upstairs when you came in is called Malcolm. He's married to Leslie and has a kid called Dustin. He put the new roof on for me. Getting him into bed was entirely my idea. And as it turned out, a good one."

Gradually, a portrait of the indolent and good-natured Diane emerged. She had married Pelling when she was young and innocent. He was a bit weird, even then, but Diane was no brainbox, nor did she consider herself a beauty. In the opinion of the Young Conservatives, to which they both belonged, it was a good match. Pretty quickly he became a District Councillor. He had discovered in himself, or so he thought, a talent for politics. By this means she met quite a few party celebs whose wives were well on the way to going barking mad. Conference was particular hell. It was a relief to get pregnant.

"For a time it was quite fun, I suppose. Tony tried to get a nomination to a parliamentary seat. He tried three times in fact. The last time, when they turned him down in some dire place in Lancashire, he took his bat home and set about making some serious money. I started screwing around."

"How old was Melissa then?"

"Oh, ten or so."

"How old was she when you and Pelling split up?"

"Seventeen?"

"And what did she make of it?"

"Search me," Diane said, suddenly gloomy. She pushed her specs back up on her nose and sat staring at the flames of the fire. When she turned slightly I saw to my astonishment she was crying.

"Pitiful, isn't it?"

"Have you seen her since you left your husband?"

"Once. I got her to come to Majorca with me in the summer. As you saw in the photographs."

"And when she got back, she did a bunk?"

"I bought her the bikini and a hundred quid's worth of clothes. I thought she might loosen up a bit. And she was improving. You know she wanted to go to Oxford, to read History?"

She wiped her cheeks on the sleeve of her sweatshirt.

"And where is she now?" I asked.

"Wrong question."

There was a much better one.

"Why does your husband want her back so urgently?"

She nodded, wiping wet cheeks with the back of her wrist.

I drove for a while around the hissing country lanes to the north and east of Hertford, where the landscape is gentle and languorous, and was rewarded by finding an Adnam's pub. I sat in the freezing cold lounge looking out of the window onto ploughed fields, fallen elms, and rooks. The landlady busied herself in phoning her mother. They were having something done to the premises, it was hard to say what exactly, but only putting the whole building onto a Cape Kennedy rocket trailer and shifting it nearer the A10 could save it.

Diane had been cute to see at a glance I had no children of my own. After the divorce, my wife remarried a sixty year old knitwear designer with a Porsche and a windmill. He was a bachelor and it seemed we were none of us destined to increase the stock of human beings in the world. I often tormented myself with that. Sitting alone in pubs brought it on. It seemed there was something incomplete in me, something more grave than lack of a higher education or mastery of a second language. Had Sally and I known when we were courting there would be no children? The terrible truth was, even allowing for the flaky nature of the long ago, I had come to believe the answer was yes.

But all this would not do. As Tania of the silver stretch marks used to say when I grew maudlin in this vein, there is no use crying over spilt milk. As my wife had foreseen from the beginning, I was one of those destined to scull around aimlessly, without purpose, without direction. I had seen her second husband on afternoon television. He was an achiever. He gave off the strong musk of a *now* person. He talked with complete confidence of what women would be wearing a year hence. They would be wearing his designs.

"You're nuts," Tania said. "The guy is a complete tosser. He probably cries himself to sleep at night."

"How d'you know I don't?"

"You! Put you in bed with a woman for an evening and you think you're made up for life. Your mother has a lot to answer for. You old fraud."

"But you've got kids, Tania. Great kids."

25

"You could have kids. All it takes, my love, is a little realism. There's plenty of women would snap you up. Give you a couple of kids and drive themselves barmy trying to get you to mow the lawn or fix the washing machine."

"You're depressing me."

"You're not a puzzle. You're good in bed, in an old-fashioned sort of way, and that's made you spoiled. And a dreamer. And about as reliable as a chocolate teapot."

I bought another pint at the bar and suppressing all this self-examination, asked myself a simple question. What would I have done in Anthony Pelling's shoes? Or Diane's?

I like to think I would have tried a little harder. In some ways, a missing person is simply a person sought by somebody else. The searchers are the story. While it was possible to imagine Melissa walking down some High Street with her nose pierced and her hair dyed mauve, leading a gaunt dog on a rope leash, it was equally possible to imagine her ordering pineapple and cottage cheese at London Weekend. Either way, in her way of looking at it, she might not be missing at all. She might be just where she always wanted to be. But then again, she might be dead. She might be on her back in a clump of blackthorn, her mouth stopped with leaves.

And now I did a very stupid thing. I walked to the payphone of the pub and rang Judith's number, something I had vowed never to do again, as long as I lived. She answered after only three rings.

"It's me," I said.

There was a very long silence.

"Where are you?"

"At the edge of a ploughed field, drinking Adnam's."

"I told you a thousand times, I never want to hear from you again."

"How are you, Judith?"

Another finely timed silence.

"I thought you were in Yorkshire screwing some unlucky bitch up there."

"I was. How's the publishing business?"

"I am not a publisher, I am an office receptionist."

"Well, how's the receptionist business?"

"Go to hell," she said, putting down the phone; or more likely, cutting the call with a stab of her finger's end. I rang her back.

"I'm sorry," I said.

This time she didn't even answer. The line went dead immediately. My eyes were smarting and my heart pounded. I felt guilty and ridiculous all at the same time. Judith was from the past. Judith had nothing to do with any of this. Any of me.

I drove back into Ware and looked for the second most consoling experience of the lonely man, a betting shop. When I found one – and it took some finding – the door was partially blocked. Some luckless old fella had collapsed shortly before the Novice Hurdle at Uttoxeter and was stretched out on the chipped floor tiles. Punters had to step over him and the two-man ambulance crew to enter. The paramedics crouched over him in grey-blue pullovers while the betting shop watched aghast and uneasy. In time, the traffic from their personal radios mingled with the race commentary. Nobody could bear to look into that corner. At last they stretchered the old man away.

Palo Doro won the race at 16-1. A pretty girl came out from behind the counter and was wiping up a little yellow puddle with a box of tissues.

"Spoils your bloody day," a burly punter said to me, uneasily. "Who was he, d'you know?"

"A missing person," I said.

Out there, in what my father was always wont to call the

27

real world, the Syrians were getting uppity and the Russians nervous. The President of the United States was good and angry and getting ready to kick ass all over again. What had to be done must be done. Out there, the trigger fingers were itchy as all hell and the walls of the interrogation centres were running with blood. Compared to all that, what was one more old guy flattened to the floor by a jolting muscle of the heart? Or come to that, the disappearance of one more middle class kid who couldn't bluff it out the way the rest of us have to?

I left, thinking of Judith and wishing myself cloud, or grass, or smoke.

THREE

Pelling rang the guest house where I was staying. It was preprandial sherry time at Pelling Towers, doubtless; at Mrs Gaskin's there was a smell of chip fat about to combust and an almost tangible acrimony in the air. La Gaskin was in a bad mood. I had come in gloomy and her other male guest had reeled through the door having drunk a shedful that afternoon at the Golf Club. His order book was empty but the booze was coming out of his ears. He was a large and prematurely bald man in his thirties with an uproarious Tyneside laugh. He found even the littlest things funny, so that he knocked the woman's barometer off the wall in an effort to remove his waxed jacket, the whole house shook. The only other residents were two young teachers, about as threatening as sugar mice. They were watching *Neighbours* and pretending Gareth was invisible.

"Good news," Pelling mumbled. "I have actually heard from Melissa today, and all's well."

"Grand," I said, seeing my fee fly out of the window. "May I ask, did you speak to her yourself, or was the call taken by one of your staff at the house?"

He chewed on that one for a few moments.

"My housekeeper took the call at home, yes."

"Did Melissa leave a return number?"

"No," Dad said slowly. "But what exactly is it that you're trying to say?"

"I don't know. You must feel sorry she didn't ring the office. I mean that must be a big disappointment for you, not to have talked to her personally."

"I am merely relieved that she's safe and well."

"But remains out of touch."

"She has *been* in touch," Pelling pointed out with maddening calm.

I stared at a little pencil drawing above the phone in the hall. It was of an angel, but one with pouting lips. Had one of the teachers doodled it? I felt sick as a parrot all round.

"Well, that is great," I said.

"I thought I should tell you all this straight away to save putting you to any more trouble."

"The case is closed, as we say?"

"I am completely reassured she is in no danger, yes."

"And what parent can say that, these days?"

He did not like my facetious side, and I could hear his lips curling. Mrs Gaskin listened at the door to the kitchen.

"If you call in at the office tomorrow, we can square our account. I am grateful to you for all you've done. Ask for my secretary, Mrs Williams. And once again, thank you."

"I would like to take it a shade further than an unconfirmable telephone call to your housekeeper, Mr Pelling."

Pelling laughed. It was clearly something he reserved for the absurdities of life, as when a servant of Pelling interests expressed a personal point of view. The laugh was all pain and disbelief.

"You really don't seem to have been listening. If you want

30

to be quite certain of how you stand in this, see my secretary in the morning. She will make it abundantly clear. And good night."

When he rang off, I stayed staring at the angel sketched on the white space of a taxi company business card. She had little breasts and a halo. Mrs Gaskin came out of the kitchen, looking truculent.

"It's pizza tonight, you know," she said, making it into a challenge for the soul of the universe.

"Count me out. Something's come up."

"And what might that be?"

"Mischief, Mrs Gaskin. Mischief."

And so it seemed. This had the prints of Pilar all over it or I was Jan Van der Luys: it was just too much of a coincidence other wise. Or maybe I was just feeling grumpy about losing the job. I had planned a day out in Cambridge in the hire car. Cambridge was nice, Cambridge was on the world map. It was just the sort of place I should be seen drinking. Since I was last there, they had opened a jazz club in Rose Cresent and that was my speed, too.

I went upstairs to fetch my coat. Gareth, the rep, was throwing up lustily in the bedroom next to mine. In between, he was laughing like a maniac. Mrs Gaskin came upstairs at the run and began banging on the door. Her husband, she said, had had enough. Big Gareth roared his appreciation and shouted something obscene through the door. Mr Gaskin, as we all knew, was a weasel of a man who could be thrashed within an inch of his life by either of the two teachers, Wend and Trace.

I rang Diane Pelling from a call box opposite the guest house and suggested she might like to go for a drink. She countered by suggesting I fetch a takeaway and have the drink at her place.

31

If anything, it was raining more fiercely than ever and wild winds were whipping up the waters of the broken pavements. I drove into Hertford and found a Tandoori takeaway with an askew picture of Prince Charles, taken in happier days.

The boy behind the counter was studying electronics and wanted to talk about smart weapons. On television, life went on, all merry and bright. Lovable little animals popped out of sand-dunes and twitched their ears. When they were at it, it looked so comical, so nice. Little Ken pushing little Pammie into position, his winkie area against her chubby bot-bot. There ought to be more television like this, the rubbish they get on these days.

"Could you make a bomb fly down one of those burrows?"

"Oh yes," the boy said enthusiastically. "You could signature the animals so that it found them wherever they were. No problem."

"Keep up the good work."

"You like these animals?"

"They remind me of something."

The boy giggled and passed me the food in a brown paper bag. The Peshwari nans were sealed into their silver bags, piping hot.

Diane had done some tidying up. The place looked warm and cosy and so did she. She was almost at the end of her first bottle of Bourgogne. When I came in, she was listening to Busoni and knitting her preposterous tam o' shanter. I dried my trouser legs in front of a blazing log fire and at her suggestion, took off my shoes and stuffed them with pages of the local free paper. She poured me a huge glass of wine.

"Your old man says he's heard from Melissa."

She hesitated, uncertain how to respond to that. It was a

curious moment. I noticed that she had made up her eyes. It made her look just that touch more guarded.

"So, a wild goose chase for you," she said.

"If what Pilar says is true. She took the call."

"Let's eat," Diane suggested, far too casually.

My gloom should have intensified. Ungallant as it may seem, while we turned out the biryiani onto blue patterned plates, I was wondering whether or not to go back to little Tania and her plump duvet under the eaves. There were really two problems: whether to go back at all, and if yes, whether to drive back in the rental car, and stick the odious Pelling with the bill.

Down here in cloud cuckoo-land, something was smelling up the place and it wasn't cardamom. On the other hand, I wasn't being paid for acting curious, or feeling sensitive. As from the time of Pelling's phone call, I wasn't being paid at all.

"It's no use looking daggers at me," Diane chided, as we munched. "I didn't ask you to come down here and poke your nose in."

"That's the distraught mother in you speaking, is it?"

"Oh dear. Are we very annoyed?"

I thought I would try to find something to say that was shrewd and intelligent, that gave the lie to the holes in my socks and woebegone slacks. I would try to astonish her with my percipience.

"Let's put it this way. What does Melissa know about you or your husband that you would rather not have revealed?"

"Nothing," Diane said.

"Try again."

"What could she know – what is there to know?"

"Your husband is probably a fine fellow deep down, but he has the warmth and approachability of fish on a slab. You look pretty okay to me in this light and you gave the kid a holiday, at least. But when she decides to get in touch, she doesn't ring Mum, she rings Pilar the Impossible at a time when she knows Dad will be raking in the coin at his place of business. It stinks."

"Everything stinks. You should know that. And anyway, you don't like people enough to care, one way or the other."

"Thank you," I said, outraged.

"You don't come round here lecturing me, you bastard."

"I wasn't lecturing."

"But you don't like people."

"Are you telling me or asking me?"

She pushed her plate away and put her head in her hands.

It came out in long pauseless sentences, as though she had been saying all this in her mind for months, behind a dam wall that had just broken. The trip to Majorca had been much more complex than Diane described. To begin with, Melissa tried to run away at the airport and when she was found and returned by the security staff, she refused to board the plane. Her mother bought her a large brandy and cajoled her into going, jeered by the other passengers; all through the flight she was terrified to let go of her daughter's hand for an instant. They consequently drank themselves silly, the two of them. An astute stewardess got the captain to radio ahead for an ambulance and they were whisked through the formalities and taken to a private clinic. There it was discovered that Melissa was pregnant.

"She was examined by this terrific man, a Jordanian. He asked her out of the blue, and she told him. Then he came in and told me."

"And could you get her to talk about it?"

"For four days we sat in the damn hotel room with the blinds drawn. We said nothing to each other – I don't suppose

34

we spoke more than a dozen words. We didn't sleep, we didn't even undress. We were on the third floor and from eight in the morning you could hear people swimming in the hotel pool. And laughing. I never let her out of my sight. They sent the food up room service. At night there were these huge electrical storms out to sea. The lightning lit the room."

"Was it so awful, what she had done?"

Diane looked at me long and hard.

"I thought it would kill her, my having found out. We just sat there sweating and stinking. On the Monday morning, I got hold of her by the wrist and dragged her into the bathroom. We sat in the shower and howled like babies. She made me promise not to tell her father – in fact I wrote out the words as a form of contract on a bit of hotel stationery. And then she got into bed and slept for a day and a half."

"How about you?"

"Went down to the bar and slept with my head on the counter."

I threw another log on the fire and fiddled about with the flames for a few moments.

"Whose was it, the child?"

"She wouldn't tell me. I asked, I begged. But she would say nothing."

"You got her to enjoy what was left of the holiday and when she got home, back to Tony's, she ran away?"

"You've got the picture," Diane said, stony faced.

"Did she run away to have an abortion?"

"She ran away."

I took the cork out of another bottle. For a long while there was just the sound of the logs spitting and the squalls of rain on the windows. Diane lay with her arms folded over her face, as if to shut out the world. I was left to stare at a picture above the fireplace, showing a shabby square in Italy. By a trick of

35

positioning, the shadow that ran diagonally through the picture was continued on the wall and ran all the way down to a little reading lamp, balanced on half a dozen books. This happy accident was in fact deeply disturbing – I wanted to get up and move the lamp. But instead I put on my shoes.

"We are one fucked up family," Diane said, abject.

I was already quite drunk enough to lose my licence if I was breathalysed on the way home. I walked into the kitchen and put my head under the tap. The water ran round my collar and trickled down my back. My teeth ached and my eyes were popping, but I was on the home stretch. Diane stared at me.

"What do you want me to say?" she asked with telepathic understanding.

"I want you to say you're worried about her."

"I'm her mother for Christ's sake," she screamed. She threw her glass at the wall and lurched to her feet. The bottle of wine rolled over regretfully and began to glug on the carpet.

"She didn't ring him today, I know that. I'm not stupid. And they are scared shitless you will find out something, yes. I don't know what. They want rid of you. He hired you, and she talked him out of it."

"Could that happen?"

"She could make him lick the cheese from between her toes."

I saw that the reason she had stood was to find the brandy, which was hiding behind some sheet music on the piano. I crossed the room and took the bottle from her. It was quite a little wrestling match but I won. In the struggle my hand brushed against her surprisingly firm breast.

"One last question. Do you think either Pilar or your husband know that she was pregnant? Or that she might even have the baby now, on her knee somewhere?"

"No, they don't. I thought I would like you, but now I find

I don't like you. I want you to go."

She took the brandy back from me without an argument and staggered to the door, knocking over a sofa table on which the television rested. It fell to the floor with a crash, followed by a second crack of sounds as the door slammed behind her.

I tidied the cushions, put the fire guard in front of the fire, poured salt over the wine stain on the carpet. I took the oily dishes into the kitchen and washed up, throwing away the silver trays and the carrier from the takeaway. Upstairs she was throwing things at the wall.

Judith once said to me, long after I had pulled her back from the gates of hell just as she was about to pass through, that I was someone who did not understand the word respect. I knew what she meant by it all right – she meant leaving people be, respecting their misery. That fitted her situation and she found it both irksome and humiliating to have anyone say they loved her enough to want to save her. She was beyond all that. And though we manufactured a quarrel in the end – it was a screaming match in a wine bar in Holland Park Road – the occasion was really only a formality. The respect she wanted from me was to mind my own bloody business. I just let go of her hand and watched her drift off into the blue beyond.

I made coffee and pulled all the wallets of photographs from Diane's shelf. Though there were eight of them, they contained no more than a dozen recent snaps of Melissa. Her life in pictures was desperately ordinary. She was a baby in a shawl, she rode a tricycle down a muddy path. Here she was captured holing out at some clock golf lawn by the sea, her hair worn in a long pigtail. She sat under a willow with her feet in a stream, Goose Cottage in the background. As a pubescent child, she stood in too-tight shorts and too-small T-shirt, her back to a wall.

There were just three taken more recently, in addition to the ones taken in Majorca. She was at some sort of civic dinner in a shoulderless evening dress, her father beside her. It was probably his idea of a great night out, but Melissa looked ready to eat the table decorations. The old sot on her other side was staring down her cleavage with a faintly aghast expression. He wore a chain of office and might even have been Mr Mayor. In the second photograph she was standing in dappled sunshine under a tree, wearing one of those wide baggy T-shirts and a cotton skirt blown by the wind. She looked fat and uncomfortable. And lastly she sat in the chair I was sitting in now, asleep. Her head was turned and her hands lay loose. Her glasses perched on the arm of the chair. I wondered idly why they had never persuaded her to have contact lenses.

The other photographs were of Diane and her husband, their friends, and – most probably – their respective parents. Pelling, from the evidence before me, had been born wearing a collar and tie. Diane, as the years rolled by, exposed more and more flesh, and to hell with the cellulite. There were a great many of those holiday snaps that just *have* to be taken, but which when processed, reveal the sea as a piece of silver paper partly enclosed by what looks like mouldy cake. There were romantic tracks leading through the olives and cute cats sitting on doorsteps beside pots of geraniums. It was all as depressing as hell.

The lady of the house came down in her torn nightie, look-ing dangerous, a glass in her hand. Her legs were sturdy and a pleasantly round belly pushed out the cotton below her comforting breasts. She scratched herself absent-mindedly.

"I thought I asked you to leave," she said.

"Ask me again."

She motioned me out of the chair – her chair – and sat

down in it with a sigh of cushions. Brandy trickled over her fingers.

"I love her," she said. "It's too late now, but I love her. That's what I came downstairs to tell you. She's a complete owl and as stubborn as all fall down, but I trust her, too. You think I'm a cow not to worry about her more. Maybe I am. But I'm a defeated woman and once you believe that, nothing you do or say can change anything."

"Whoever told you you were defeated was a man. Never trust a man in matters of victory and defeat. An old Chinese proverb. Are you going to be all right?"

"Is this your gallant bit you're giving me now?"

"I'm still smarting over the misanthropy you think you find in me."

"Oh shut up," Diane said. Under her nightie she wore raggy purple knickers with the hem unstitched. "Put some music on and don't be such a scold."

In the end I opened another bottle and we sat listening to Dinah Washington while the wind roared in the chimney. I told her about Judith, and how I lost her, and what I wanted from life, which was for someone to discover another manuscript by Mencken, tucked away in some tin trunk in Baltimore by one of his musical buddies before the great wordsmith lost his powers of speech. But Mencken was just another name to Diane, and anyway, I was lying. Or fooling myself. What I wanted was somehow to be transmogrified into a cheery paterfamilias who had never heard of Mencken but was a whiz at making the kids laugh and a pillar of the village adult education group. I wanted a long low house up a muddy lane in Lincolnshire with really terrific perennials growing in the borders of the garden.

After some difficulty with a third bottle, and well into the early hours, I left her asleep, as probably the only other way to get rid of me. I covered her with a crocheted patchwork quilt, switched off the lights, put the fireguard back on sentry duty, kissed her on the unfeeling cheek and stumbled out into the dark.

The rain had left off and a stiff gale was blowing across the flooded meadows, whipping up the water into little dancing waves. I fell over on my way to the car and lay gasping in the juicy gravel. My heart was pounding and I could feel each tooth as a separate item in my head. And, like Gareth, the laughing rep, I found myself corpsing gently, almost too drunk to stand, and too miserable to care. In such circumstances, if you didn't laugh, you'd cry.

FOUR

Pilar was taking a sauna in the dinky little gymnasium he had set up for her in the cellars. Her robe was purest cotton, decorated with a Chinese red initial. She smelled of cedar and lemons – not the juice, the zest of lemons. With her hair slicked back and no shoes or make-up, she looked about seventeen years old. She received me in the hall. The cleaning lady who had let me in was hoovering away vigorously in the study, no doubt reflecting on those families who had saunas and studies, and those who had not. Pilar seemed uncertain what to say or do.

"Your money is waiting for you at the office, I think."

"I wanted to say goodbye."

She opened her eyes wide, like a film star mugging an emotion she could not feel.

"I'll come clean. I came to ask you how to find Melissa. On my own account, If you like, for my own gratification. Then I'll go."

She made a face and set off wordlessly back down to the gym. I followed. By the time I got there, she was in the shower, behind peach tinted glass panels. Once on a while, a little

41

moon of her flesh pressed against the steamy panels. It was quite hard to bear in mind that outside were the bleak and empty streets of a commuter town in mid-morning.

"This is all very nice in here," I called, motioning at all the machinery scattered about on the spongy floor. Pelling had spent a bomb on keeping her healthy. "Does Master go for a row on this thing, or maybe he cycles to Welwyn Garden City and back on the exercise bike? Nothing like keeping in trim. And what about Melissa? Did she like to keep fit too, in her girlish way? There's enough junk in here to beef her up for a trial with the London Broncos."

The shower ceased and Pilar stepped out, gesturing for me to pass her the robe. Though she was half turned away from me, she made no attempt to be coy. Apart from her eyes, she looked delicately tinted, pert and innocent. Her eyes looked hot and dangerous.

"Okay. How much do you want?"

"What a strange thing to say."

"I haven't got time for games. Just name your price and clear off."

"You're not playing this scene too well, Pilar."

"I'll give you a thousand pounds to clear off and mind your own business."

"Do you know if she had the baby?" I asked with artful casualness.

The housekeeper stared at me. Christ, I was having a field day – hungover, broke and nowhere near as clean as she, giving her a bad time in her own damn gymnasium. Some of this communicated itself.

"You frighten me," she said slowly.

"About Melissa. She didn't ring yesterday, did she?"

"Yes."

"You know damn well she didn't. You told Pelling what he

wanted to hear. Maybe because you're so fond of the big goof. Or maybe to stop him from finding out the truth. This grand you're offering me – that'd be your own money, would it?" She took a comb from the pocket of her robe and dragged it through her hair. The cellar windows had dinky Venetian blinds which would have cast a barred light over us had we been in the movie. Pilar licked her lips.

"Wait upstairs for me while I dress," she said.

Out of deference to the gods of the hearth, I waited in the garden, smoking and dead-heading the flowers in Pelling's borders. The cleaning lady was watching me out of the window, and got her reward when Pilar came out wearing a leather jacket not much smaller than a settee and certainly using up as much cow. On her head she had jammed one of Master's trilbies, and it suited her. In fact she looked delicious.

We drove in the rental to a pub in Norman's Cross. It was one of those places where the bar staff are haughty girls in blinding white T-shirts with names like Kate or Jools. She asked for a white wine spritzer and I took a pint of Old Predictable. We sat in a corner behind a sprawling avocado in a fancy pot. Some ancient bit of farm machinery hung on the wall behind our heads, decorated with wisps of designer hay. Perhaps in olden times this was where the ploughman sat to eat his lunch. Our entrance had turned a few heads – she had a composure that came from riches and that always plays well in pubs like this. Her breasts jiggled about inside a grey silk polo neck and she wore fabulous white trousers supported by one of Pelling's club ties, the waistband turned over in a sort of gamine insouciance. She refused the offer of a meal and lit a pink paper cigarette with a tiny grimace of disgust.

"Pink not your colour?"

"Anthony has begged me a hundred times to stop smoking," she said absently.

"It's exciting for him. The struggle for control of your lungs, your hidden organs. Are you really his housekeeper?"

"I have a salary and a flat. There is sex, obviously – he's not that stupid. It's not all cooking and laundry."

"How did you meet him?"

"I've told you, we met in London."

"And this grand you want to give me, what's the story behind that?"

"You show signs of being the kind of creep that rings up the tabloids."

"Unless you've buried her in the garden, I don't think the tabloids are going to get too excited. What's your thousand pound secret, Pilar?"

"I'm ambitious," she said, brief and to the point.

I thought about it. The simplicity of the remark had a certain appeal. If she had ambition, it ran no further than the sort of complacency indicated by the conversations going on around us. They were mostly in their sixties, our neighbours, tucking into their boeuf bourguignon and leek pie, sublimely confident that everything was tickety-boo. The plateau of their contentment stretched away like the Russian steppe. Mandy and Peter were coming for Christmas, the Anstruthers were doing were doing their usual drinks thing on New Year's Eve, Bob and Jane were going back to Cyprus for the third year running. And wasn't it priceless that Jeremy could actually make money teaching English to the Japanese when he had been more or less expelled from St Olaf's for being so dull? It was really too much.

Pilar wanted to belong to all this, to the drawled mediocrities and aimless pauses of Pelling's clients and friends. She wanted to front up as the second Mrs P, live in a big house, run her own Mercedes and fly off to Tenerife when here in England the snow lay all around deep and crisp and even. She

44

wanted to buy her clothes in South Moulton Street and forget she ever saw the cabs splashing through the sewage in Manila.

"Will he marry you, do you think?"

She gave me a long and level look.

"I don't see why not. He's greedy. In certain ways."

"So did *you* sling Melissa out?"

"He did. She went away to have an abortion, you've worked that out, I imagine. She went to Cambridge, where he has friends. It was all set up in Cambridge, but she didn't come home. At first he was worried, and then he sort of put it out of his mind. Then his mother died."

"Oh yes?"

"Melissa inherited quite a lot of money."

"Give me a clue."

"Half a million," she said, poker faced.

I went to the bar to order her a prawn sandwich. It was prepared before my eyes by the haphazard and preoccupied Kate (or was it Jools?) who was nattering to Jools (or was it Kate?) about the best places to go dancing in Miami. This conversation took place as though I were not present at all. The thing about Miami was that it was really naff, but you could always fly up to New Orleans for a couple of days. Or people who had boats could take you to the Keys. Such people would be child molesters, or otherwise desperate characters, no doubt. I thought about Melissa on the hoof somewhere, with half a million burning a hole in some solicitor's safe. No wonder Dad wanted her back for a chat on wise investment.

"I *said*," Kate-or-Jools ground out, with heavy emphasis, "that'll be two-ninety."

When I walked the sorry-looking, drooling mess back to Pilar she did not hesitate. Taking it from my hand, she went back to the bar with springy step.

"What the hell do you call this? And don't bother to

45

answer. Go and fetch me someone in charge of the kitchens, and that means right away."

And it worked. Wherever she had laid her head in London, in whatever hotel, Pilar had learned the knack of reducing people to a crisp. There was a flurry of activity and harsh words were spoken on our side. The publican, who wore a beard and a piratical earring, as well as a viridian green bow tie, practically wept with shame. Pilar walked back to the table behind the avocado, her tongue behind her top teeth, eyes flashing. Our neighbours liked her for it. People suddenly discovered that their knives had not been quite clean, and that the girls were really rather tiresome. Viridian Bow Tie came over with a state-of-the-art prawn sandwich and a glass of champagne for the lady.

"What a bunch of pricks," Pilar muttered.

"You were saying: half a million."

"His father owned a company that made plaster board. That old bitch was loaded, believe me."

Having the fight about the sandwich seemed to have loosened Pilar up quite a bit; or maybe she felt that in me she was dealing with a loser, and so had no special need to dissemble.

"Tell me about the Cambridge connection."

"She isn't there."

"No, but tell me all the same."

"He belongs to some supper club. They dine once a fortnight. It has nothing to do with it. Tony went to Christ's, I think. He likes to think he's still in touch."

"Does Melissa know she's rich – I mean did she know she was going to inherit?"

"We'd have had a different story otherwise," Pilar said dryly.

"You mean from Pelling. He'd have shown a bit more interest in her."

"For half a million? I think so."

It was pretty electrifying, the terse way she grasped the this-and-that of family finance. I suddenly had a very different picture of them in bed together. After Diane, with her casual approach to life, her torn nighties and her chunky hips, screwing Pilar would seem to Tony like an intellectual challenge not even a Cambridge supper club could match. When she was fully on song, I could imagine Pilar as the Philippine Lady Macbeth.

"You don't want him to find her because you know who gave her the baby."

It was an inspired guess. Pilar laughed, and the whole damn pub looked at us with envy and admiration. In the undemanding ambiance of the Fox and Hounds, we were somebody. It helped that she had yet to take off his trilby and that laughing set her breast in merry motion in a way that was – for the elderly male punters watching – an early Christmas peal of bells. But the laugh in no wise meant she was going to tell me who the father was of Melissa's child. It meant that she was not.

"You're not going to be a good boy and shove off, are you?"

"I haven't asked you for the thousand pounds either," I pointed out.

"And that's something you may live to regret," Pilar said, feeling she had the ascendancy of a man who can't even get the prawn sandwich he ordered.

When I got back to the Primlea Guest House it chanced that Malcolm, Diane's randy roofer, was waiting for me in his van. There was actually little of chance in it – he had been driving past the guest house earlier in the day when I was reversing out. The lad was confused and angry enough about something to come back later and wait for me. He had passed the time reading the *Mirror* propped up on the steering wheel and smoking rollies as though they were going out of fashion. And by the time we met he was psyched up to a concert pitch of dangerous thoughts.

"Don't you feel the cold?" I asked, indicating his T-shirt.

But he was not in the mood to exchange pleasantries about the weather. He was there to give me his youthful truculence, his imminent grievous bodily harm, an act he had honed in many a solitary session down at the boozer.

"I want to know what your game is, pal, and don't try messing me about."

I took pity on him, the poor kid, with his flat stomach and bulging biceps. I let him off lightly.

"Take me to a pub, big Mal, and I'll buy you a pint."

"Wha'?"

"A pint."

We drove in his van to a huge roadhouse on the old A10 and sat in the cheerless lounge, glowering at each other. We were the only customers. A gay barman was practising pool shots. Malcolm rolled me a cigarette, looking suddenly careworn and vulnerable. He had a haircut that cost him a few notes and a gold chain round his neck but was otherwise, as he confided, up shit creek. The weather, the government and his wife were all killing him. Some days, like today, he drove about from pub to pub on the pretence of being at work and then drove home to eat fish fingers and backed beans with his kids, wishing himself dead. His wife suspected he was having it off with someone. That was the point of our meeting.

"How come?"

"She's hired you to effing spy on me, that's how come."

"That's a big flattery you're paying yourself, Mal. I'm expensive. I'm international class when it comes to money.

48

Your wife couldn't afford me."

"You don't know her," he cried. "She's completely out of order on this jealously thing. If you are sloofing me, it's her that's done it."

"Sloofing?" I asked, bemused.

"Me and Mrs Pelling."

She was called Leslie, the jealous wife, and she sounded a bit of a case, with her daily inspection of his underpants and her well-hard brother in the Dragon Guards. At first it had all gone beautifully. They met on poxy holiday in Malaga and followed things up at the Redondo Beach, Welwyn Garden City. Leslie bonked like a dream and earned good money as a temp. Then, three months pregnant and thus a bit late in the day from Barbara Cartland's point of view, she took him home to meet the family. Roger, the brother, was one of those six foot five squaddies whose hands were killing instruments. Her parents were the surprise – they worked the pubs as a musical duo, playing sixties hits. That should have been the warning. Leslie had the show business in her veins.

After lumbering herself and him with a couple of kids, a right couple of ankle-biters, she began to show her restless streak. She was a belter in the Randy Crawford style and had auditioned for TV talent shows. She even had an agent in Broxbourne. In short, like Pilar but in a different way, she was ambitious.

"He's nobbing her, that's certain," Malcolm said darkly.

"Who? The agent? Your problems are not my problems, sunshine. I'm not following you. I'm looking for Diane's daughter. Simple as that."

He laughed for the first time. The tone was richly derisive.

"How much is it worth?"

"You mean you know where she is?"

"I know a few things about Melissa."

"Things you haven't told Diane?"

"I never even mentioned her to Diane."

"That wouldn't be the Christian way, would it?"

"Piss off," Malcolm said, growing more cheerful by the minute. He walked to the bar to buy me a drink. I wondered whether he was jerking me around, but decided he was too innocent of life. He carried back the pints with a light step.

"Is there any money in this?"

"For you, old son? No. What there is, I go see Diane and tell her you've been holding out on her and it's no more bacon sandwiches in bed for you."

"Fat lot I care," he said, but tinged with regrets.

The story was not as complex as I had imagined. It seemed that Leslie's agent was a Mr Sanderson, who ran his business from a little greengrocer's shop near the *Flag* in Broxbourne. Malcolm felt sure I knew it. Mr Sanderson had several warblers on his books in addition to Leslie, as well as some multi-instrumental freak called Billy and a few wan kids who played keyboards and worked weddings and old folks' homes.

"And then he has the other stuff," Malcolm said.

"Oh yes?"

"You, know, the photographic models. It's dead ordinary, like. He advertises in the free paper. They're not slags or anything like that. But it's an earner for him. I done work for him on his garage roof and that's how I know."

"And where does Melissa fit into this?"

He stared, as though I was stupid.

"She worked there. You know, modelled."

My jaw hung open.

"Part-time," Malcolm said helpfully. "While she was at school and that."

"Melissa worked part time at a photographic studio in Broxbourne? We're talking *nude* modelling?"

"That's the biz."

"*Before* she did a bunk?"

"Yeah," he said.

"And what else? You said you know a few things."

He rubbed his thumb and finger together briskly under my nose.

"Twenty," he said. "Just for a drink on the way home."

"Don't give me that. If you're not home in ten minutes Leslie'll be chucking the electric fire into the bath after you. You're not boxing your own weight here, Mal. Just tell me and get it over with."

"All right. I got this friend, he's rewiring this house for these rich geezers and his mate, his oppo, has pissed off with the van and all the dosh. So I'm helping him out, like. It' s an old house and we have to chase the wiring back into the wall in some rooms, the attic rooms. It comes out the ark, that wiring. You never saw a board like it, or I never have. So I'm labouring for him, like, and I come to the house one morning and who should I see, bollock naked? Melissa!"

"Where?"

"In bed."

"No, *where*, you dick?"

"Kentish Town," he said.

"When?"

"In the summer."

"Was she staying with the people, as a house guest or something?"

"Yeah, possibly," Malcolm said with a sneer. "Two blokes in their seventies? In a shithole like that?"

"What sort of two blokes?"

"Find out for yourself, pal."

"Now you're giving me a hard time, Mal. I don't want to get heavy with you."

"You!" he scoffed.

"You saw her in bed. Was she drugged?"

"Piss off," he said, much more cheerful now that it was likely to come down to his physique over mine.

But then he was a child in these matters. Walking back to the van, I touched his arm, and when he turned, still good-humoured, still full of bounce and about to give me his awful warning about having boxed for Hertfordshire or some such rubbish, I hit him with my forearm across the windpipe. He fell to the gravel like a sack of coals. I dragged him in the lee of the van, away from the pub windows and sat him up against the rear wheel arch. My hand closed lightly over the bulge in the front of his jeans.

"Now I've got a bit of your future in my hand here, big Malcolm, and if you're feeling rough now, that's nothing to how you're going to feel in the next thirty seconds. I'm old, but I'm dirty with it."

"I can't breathe," he whistled and croaked. "You mad-arse bastard."

"*Don't* breathe," I advised.

So now I'm some big-shot avenging angel beating up a boy with a thirty quid haircut in a pub yard. It did the business with Malcolm all right, but scared the hell out of me. I helped him into the van and he gave me the keys. We drove to the Chequers in Ware and I bought him a rum and coke.

Melissa had been naked in the way people are when they sleep with no clothes on. Far from being drugged, she had been sitting up in bed reading the paper and eating a bowl of corn flakes when he saw her. He did not know she was Diane's daughter at the this time and had yet to meet Diane. She was just a plump girl from whom he tried – unsuccessfully – to cadge a cigarette. He had no idea of her identity. That made me feel bad about whacking him for a moment or so; but not much longer than that. He was touching his throat with his fingertips and scowling at me; but I knew he could also feel the hook loosen in his mouth. I was not going to do him more physical harm.

"You're a bloody nutter, you," he said.

"I surprised myself," I said. "And that's the truth. This kid is in danger, maybe. And meanwhile you and Diane are in clover."

"Yeah? What about the dad and his bit on the side?"

"I feel like hitting all of you, the way it is tonight. You bastard, Malcolm. In time, didn't Diane show you photographs – holiday snapshots – of Melissa? And didn't you recognise her from those?"

"Not straight away."

"But you did make the connection, you berk."

"Yes."

"And you said nothing."

"Why should I?" he said in a little-boy whine That was life, the way he saw it: maybe she wouldn't have thanked him for telling her where her daughter was, either. Maybe he understood that. But the pained indignation in his voice got on my nerves.

I felt a lot better about hurting him.

FIVE

Cyril Sanderson shared some physical resemblance with Melissa's father. He was very narrow of skull and long of neck. But otherwise he was out of a different box. That night he wore a flapping yellow cardigan over a check shirt and a RAFA tie. His moustache was modelled on something like a clarinet cleaning brush, an image that easily came to mind because plain Mr Sanderson (as he was now) had once been Warrant Officer Sanderson of the Band of the Royal Air Force. Serving Her Majesty for so many years on clarinet, alto and tenor had left him cautious but unafraid.

"I did actually meet Artie Shaw once when the Band was touring Germany. I went backstage to see him in Cologne. Explained who I was and that and chatted. I don't rate him the best, I don't know about you, I mean everybody laughs at Sid Phillips, but you couldn't top Sid in his heyday. People think swing music is American music and the rest of us come nowhere. Rubbish."

His wife was out, watching a pub act over in Harlow, which I think he mentioned to give me some idea of the far flung nature of the *Blue Skies Agency*. We sat in the kitchen to

54

his flat, drinking coffee made with disgusting amounts of milk. It was all very cosy. Stuck to the fridge door were photographs of his grandchildren and their dogs and tricycles. The vibes were good. Cyril seemed about as harmless as the stair carpet.

"Melissa," I prompted.

"Oh my gawd! You're not her dad, are you? You can't be. If you are I take my hat off to you. What a girl! What a complete corker that kid was!"

"Was?"

"We had to get rid of her. It was that or adoption. The wife runs the model side of the business. Sue was a mother to that poor kid. We got her some work, not much, you know a few regulars, all to be trusted."

"What sort of work?"

"Posing," he said, unembarrassed. "Modelling, if you like. It's money for old rope, really. The girls have a panic button in the studio they can press and anyway the whole thing – what they're saying while they're alone together – is being broadcast to Beryl, just to be on the safe side. We tell the punters that before the start. We don't get any dafties. All nice family men with their cameras and their little tripods. They send the girls Christmas cards, that sort of thing."

"And Melissa was a corker."

"A princess," Sanderson said fondly. "My godfathers, yes! And could she talk! Talked up a storm."

"Isn't that part of the job?"

"Yes, but not about Bismarck and all that lot. You know, whassname, Disraeli or Garibaldi. Which one do I mean?"

"Garibaldi was the one with the biscuits."

"The other one, then."

"And how did this go down with the boys?"

"Loved it! Abso-bloody-lutely adored her. See, we're dead

careful about how we carry on, that's how I know you're not from the council like you say you are. We don't exploit anyone. We have a nice class of person coming here. On both sides of the lens, so to speak. I hope you don't want to give me an argument about that."

"Just good clean fun."

He held up a long knobby finger.

"Exactly. That's just exactly what it is. You can count on my Beryl to keep it that way."

He was completely artless, our Cyril. We finished our coffee and after enquiring cautiously whether I was driving, he invited me to a can of Schlitz in the sitting room. It was probably the most illicit thing he had done that week. He explained that he heart was a bit dicky. Valves. So we sat there in these huge golden brown armchairs twinkling at each other and listening to someone he *did* rate, Buddy de Franco. His hi-fi system was surprisingly good. I had to wrench myself back to the matter in hand.

"She left you, in the end. Know what happened to her?"

He shook his head.

"Nothing terrible. That kid was flameproof, old love."

"She's missing."

"No!" Sanderson said with a surprise he could not possibly have feigned. The news made him flustered enough to light a little cheroot. He seemed genuinely anxious. His hands shook a little.

"You mean she's missing from home?"

"You don't know anything about it?"

"Me? No, I'm choked, I don't mind telling you. We were both very fond of Mels."

It seemed that when she first presented herself to the agency, Beryl had suggested she get herself some frilly knicks, something a bit peekaboo, and in that fashion disguise herself.

56

That way she would not have to bare all, and it was more like going to the doctor, or trying on a dress somewhere. Not that there was anything to be ashamed about in the human body: we all had the same bits and pieces and there were very few surprises in that department, very few indeed. Meanwhile, a pair of knicks or a g-string was as good as the Lone Ranger's mask. In a manner of speaking. Most people knew that glamour – meaning naughty lingerie and cheeky poses – was as complete a fiction in Broxbourne as in Northanger Abby.

"Good advice, really," Sanderson said. "Sounds bloody rough, the way I'm telling it, but B knows all about it – she was a good stripper in her day, up north. I don't say she made a science of it, but she knew the score, still does."

"And Melissa liked her?"

"Loved her."

It was certainly possible to imagine the loner of the Upper Sixth finding her way to Broxbourne on the train, where there was at any rate a bit of human warmth, a feeling of family.

There was much to chat about. Beryl the stripper and student of human nature had settled down in time to become a mother to Pauline, who was married to Joachim of Kaiserlauten. Grandpa showed me the pictures of his two little bundles of joy, romping in a jolly German wood. It helped his case that Joachim was a pastor. And the son of a pastor.

"You knew she was still at school, I suppose."

"At school, but eighteen. Oh yes. She turns up here, the kid, a good stone overweight and sits out there in the kitchen, doing her homework! Calm as anything. Before she's finished, she's got Beryl running around looking it all up, the Congress of Vienna or something. While she sits on a tuffet down at the old studio, gassing her head off to the punters. Bemusing them."

"Did she ever get the knicks?"

Sanderson smiled sadly. He went to a hideous drop leaf

bureau and rummaged around in the drawers. He came up with some loose ten by eights of Melissa and passed them across. I could not help smiling too as I studied them. Sanderson grinned back. We were men of the world, all right, two canny wee beggars. In the pictures, she had taken everything off except her glasses. With these firmly planted on her snub nose she had given her clients naked innocence, of the sort you might expect from a peeled boiled egg. In one pose, she sat with an elbow on her knee, her chin in her hand, leaning forward like Churchill contemplating world history. I wondered gloriously who had paid Sanderson money to hire this solid and remorseless interrogator, with her wristwatch and her frown.

"She was a lovely kid," her former employer said. "A star in her own way."

"Did she have special favourites, or did anyone make her a special?"

"Leave it out," Sanderson said sharply. "We have model booking forms and I could tell you exactly who chose her and what date. I know all the blokes by sight. I even print the bloody negs meself, some of them. Mr Lillee's a client of ours. The auctioneer from Church Road. And others. Including an old lad of ninety-two. Like I'm telling you, she was almost family. We loved her."

"She's still missing, Cyril."

"Yeah, well, more's the pity."

"And last summer, somebody got her pregnant."

His reaction astonished me. He jumped from his chair and the veins on his forehead bulged. I though with some alarm about his dicky heart.

"Right. You find that bastard that did that and I'll finish him, I swear to God. That is right out of order. You've astonished me there all right."

"You don't know anything about it?"

He looked at me with his rage unabated, his watery blues eyes cold and unfriendly.

"I may be in my sixties, mate, but I'll deck you if you give me any more of that. None of my lads could have done it. They knew: she was a daughter to me. I know a bit about where she comes from, the sort of people who are her real parents. And they don't deserve her."

In such an atmosphere, it seemed wrong to Cyril to have the images of Melissa scattered between us. Before he swept them up, I caught a glimpse of her as the Unclothed Maja, her belly rounds as a casserole, and still showing the faint marks of her underwear. She was looking off-camera and probably thinking about French colonial expansion under Faidherbe, or something of the sort.

"You say you got rid of her. How did that happen?"

"She was going on holiday with her Mum, or something."

"She was already pregnant then."

"I don't *believe* it," Sanderson said. "That is just *unbelievable*. You learn something new every day, stone me if you don't. So it comes out we persuaded her to leave just when she needed us most, does it?"

"How did it happen?"

"She was a bit shaky. She'd missed a couple of bookings—"

He paused suddenly to think about the implications of what he had said. He studied his shaking hands with a rueful expression and rubbed at the grave marks he found there with real tears filling up his eyes.

"But that wasn't it, either. Beryl just talked to her and said she was too nice for this game, which she was. Said she should think it over on holiday. We didn't want to take the money away from her, but we knew she had a bob or two behind her. And it wasn't really right. Not for her. She never came back, and so we assumed she had taken the hint."

"And you really can't say anything about the pregnancy?"

"She was upset about something, yes," he muttered, after a moment of two. "But Mels is tough, I mean really tough. I never guessed it could be that. The bastard."

"It couldn't have been anyone here? I have to ask you, Cyril."

"It's art with them, not sex. You'd have to be a bit gone at the game to see our little studio as a sex parlour. Come on, I'll show it to you. Then you'll get the picture."

It was a lock-up a few hundred yards away on a tiny little industrial unit by the revamped railway station. Inside it was all extremely orderly – and freezing cold. Beryl's gumboots were in a corner of the room, under a table on which there was a two-element Cona and a little stack of paper cups. Cyril opened the door to the studio and I peered in. It was the sort of place you might otherwise store crockery. A yellow paper cyc hung from the steel rafters. There was a white chair and a tall jardiniere with a plastic fern sprouting from it. Cyril pointed to the microphone in the ceiling.

"I used to walk her to the station myself some nights. Carry her book bag. She was done here by nine, home by a quarter to ten."

"How's Malcolm's wife Leslie?" I asked all of a sudden. Sanderson was completely unfazed. He smiled calmly and nodded.

"I wondered how you found me. Her husband tipped you, did he? Leslie's a different kettle of fish altogether. And she doesn't come into this. You'd like that, wouldn't you? But you're barking up the wrong tree, pal."

"Big Malcolm thinks you're giving her one."

"And he'd be right," Leslie's agent said laconically.

"Bit more glamour and adventure in the show business side of things, is there, Cyril?"

"What would you know about it?" Cyril said, meaning the show business, life, and being an ex-clarinet player. He closed the door of the studio and walked to the street door.

"Think what you like," he said. "I'm not Father Bloody Christmas, never said I was. Leslie's on for it and that's good enough for me. It's a mutual thing. Could hardly be otherwise. I'm not exactly Cary Grant, am I?"

We tramped back to the flat above the greengrocer's through little spats of rain, Cyril smouldering with obscure indignation. He wanted to say something brisk and cutting, but he was right, he wasn't Cary Grant. A dewdrop glistened on his adulterous nose, and he massaged his heart absentmindedly with a veined and mottled hand. He looked his years, but I could see what Leslie saw in him. He was kind and shy. I liked him.

It was still early enough to drive down to Kentish Town. I expected nothing more out of it than a pint and a fish and chip supper in the car; but what Malcolm had called sloofing is much more often time spent like that than by leaping through plate glass windows or abseiling down the side of some high rise with a knife between your teeth.

I puttered into London thinking about Melissa's idea of a little excitement. Whatever it was in the abstract, it included getting pregnant by someone and then doing a runner. But who knew her? Unless she had been raped by a stranger, to whom did she submit her mind and body; and in what unknowable place – bed or car park, golf course or lay-by?

I parked the car in a frosty little side street and walked around for a while trying to imagine someone – anyone – being admitted to Melissa's lonely world of school, and the secret modelling job and home sweet home. Once admitted, expelled – for I could not imagine him with her now somehow. He had not been waiting in the shadows outside Pelling's house, that fateful night, waiting to be asked in once Mels had spilled the beans. When she was handed a wad of notes and an address in Cambridge, there was no one to hold her hand. Nobody shook his fist in the direction of the Pelling windows before driving off with the mother-to-be. Putting it simply, Melissa had been shafted all round. And thus, I concluded, she was just what beanpole Dad said she was: missing. She was missing in that irritating and niggling way that a central piece of jigsaw goes missing. Without her, things were incomplete.

Half an hour before last orders, I turned in at one of those grey and unkempt pubs that look as grim as a Turkish prison. It was the sort of place where the brewery puts in a manager who has learned to get his retaliation in first. And the mood was ugly all right. A Karaoke Night had just concluded and the police had been called. Tough girls with berets and single breasted macs, their necks hung with silly satchels, were slagging off half an dozen building workers who had disrupted *their* disruption of 'Heard It On The Grapevine'. Someone called Anne Marie had been flattened while attempting a little number from the back catalogue of martial arts. About ten young black guys sat with their backs to the fracas as though there entirely on their own.

And in the snug, sitting side by side, two old gents who looked like elderly radio actors. They were drinking large brandies.

"Who cares about Marvin Effing Gaye?" Barry the landlord shouted, wiping thick red snot from his nose into the hem of his T-shirt. "Sit down and shut up, the bloody lot of you."

"Don't call me a lot," a termagant shouted. "I'm not a lot, you ignorant animal."

Barry had made her day, and possibly her week. She

dropped into a crouch, her hands in front of her, her Doc Martens firmly planted.

"Hai!"

"Oh shit," the landlord whined. Things were getting out of hand all over again, despite the soothing powers of 'Brown Sugar' without the treble, and loud enough to curl the lino. The girl pirouetted, posed for a second like The Skating Parson, whirled and kicked Bazza in the cods. I chose the two old gentlemen to speak to about Melissa, a craven decision, but you weren't there and didn't see Barry looking for his manhood.

"I'm looking for a girl called Melissa Pelling," I shouted.

"And you might she be?" the thinner of the two asked.

"Well, last summer she was in the district, I think. You might remember her. A big girl, plump. Eighteen. Specs."

"A lovely little word picture," he sniggered. "There can't be two people in London like that."

"Maybe she stayed at your house?"

His smile was still there, but I fancy I noticed a new respect in his eyes.

"What on earth would give you that idea?"

Malcolm was right. They were seventy if they were a day. And they had seen and heard it all before. The one who had yet to speak yawned in my face, and this despite the action in the pub, where Barry was rolling around on the floor and the girl who had kicked him was taking licks from one of the building workers. We could say of this pub that it was an anteroom to hell. In fact I did say so.

"Is it really? We've been coming here for years."

Of course: they lived just round the corner.

The thin man, the one who did all the talking, was called Peter. His partner went immediately to bed, or at any rate disappeared. Peter and I sat in a front room smelling of soot and old carpets. The atmosphere was otherwise bookish. My host served me a can of lager in a filthy glass. He poured himself another almighty brandy. For some reason there was a bicycle leaning against the wall. The tyres had perished. There was the remains of a fish and chip supper for two on the table in the window. You may well ask how any of this contributed to a bookish atmosphere. The answer was scattered in profusion all round the room. Peter and his chum were mighty readers of pulp fiction. If a best-seller is a book that you read on a plane and leave on a plane, these two were going against the trend. The busiest titles of the last twenty years were to be found in piles, in rows, singly and in heaps, like peat bricks.

"A shrewd piece of observation. We use them for just that. They are fuel, old love. We're book burners."

"Do you read them first?"

"Roger does. I used to. But you didn't come to discuss our funny little ways."

"The girl's name was Melissa Pelling," I reminded him.

"Yes."

He was hard to place. He wore rather a good suit, from the days when suits were made to last. His shoes were old-fashioned but had been most assuredly made on a bench by a man with a mouthful of tacks. His crumpled and stained tie was troubling me too until I realised it was First and Third Boat Club. But he was not donnish. There was no affectation in him, no weary cynicism. It was just possible that he had been up at Cambridge in the fragrant past, when the hair that flopped forward now, snowy-white, had been blonde and sun-kissed.

"It's as though in a way you've sprung to life from this sort of rubbish we've been burning in the grate. It's quite intriguing. I wonder what sort of detective genius you are. I can certainly hear the cogs whirring."

"Detection's not my strong point. I just stumble along the track that's most rutted. I follow the crowd."

"Well, we know what Auden said about that. Man is either a cipher in a city, or a pilgrim on a lonely road. Something like that, I can't remember exactly. But thrilling, in an undemanding sort of way. Don't you think?"

"The girl's father hired me to find her, and now he's changed his mind. Perhaps a bit too suddenly."

"Ah," he said. "Plot."

"Maybe. I'm not sure where it leaves me."

"Out in the cold I should have thought. Or are you pursuing the quarry for your own pleasure? Your sense of personal destiny. Down these mean streets and so on?"

"Was she ever here?"

He gave me a line that rocked me back on my heels.

"She's my niece, dear." he said equably. "Tony's my brother."

"You're Pelling's *brother*?"

"Try not to sound so startled. He's my half-brother. We share the same father. Or perhaps he hasn't told you."

I remembered Diane's hesitation when I asked about aunts and uncles.

"He hasn't."

"Bert Pelling – Dad, shall we call him? – was a bit of a ram, at any rate so far as Hertford worthies go. He was ninety odd when he died and still, according to the testimony of the nursing home in Hove where they had him more or less pacified, a keen enthusiast. He married Dora, first of all, and after planting her in that rather nice St Michael's in Hertford, remarried the amazing Margaret, and begat little Anthony. Who in time begat Melissa. I understand Tony's a bit of a swordsman himself. Some foreign beauty. You've met her, no doubt."

"I'm still trying to take all this on board."

"Is it specially unusual? Or sinister? The very stuff of Victorian fiction, I should have thought – or for that matter Californian fiction. Of course, in the California version I would be rather more glamorous, I think. Perhaps a film producer, or a Senator. But somebody who comes along in Chapter Five to fuck the whole thing up."

"And is that what you've done?"

"My dear old love," Peter Pelling protested faintly.

These confessions seemed to unlock his cupboard of generosity. He found a half-full bottle of single malt and threw another Jack Higgins on the fire. After a certain amount of twitching about, he managed to coax music from his battered ghetto blaster, and we sat listening to a tape of Charles Trenet. 'Moi, J'aime Le Music Hall'. I tried to imagine Melissa sitting in this room and gave up after a few minutes. Peter Pelling stayed on the brandy, for which he had the appetite of a Byron. He told me all about Roger, who had written the jingles for many a television ad in the fifties and early sixties.

"That's when we met. He was married to rather an awful woman called Pansy. She dressed and talked like Shirley Temple but was much more implacable in temperament. She painted. I can't tell you how terrible these daubs were – things like cormorants flying out of the fundament of priests and so on. Not a popular artist."

"How about you and Tony? What sort of half brothers are you?"

"I was never invited to tea, if that's what you mean. My stepmother took a dim view. And Tony's an achiever. I like

Diane, whom I've met a couple of times. And I very much like Melissa. We sent away for her horoscope, you know. It was absolutely fascinating. She shares her planets with Stalin. I thought that was priceless."

"Look, Peter, this is nice and spooky, sitting around burning books and listening to Trenet at one in the morning. But I want to finish up this business of Melissa. She inherited quite a lot of loot from your stepmother, I suppose you knew."

"More power to her elbow, old thing."

"Yes, indeed, but that also puts you in the frame, as someone who presumably did not benefit from the will. Or not as grandly as she."

"Benefitted not at all. Without wishing to, either. All that Hertford thing is a very long time ago. I can vaguely see what you're trying to do. You think this is a family affair. I suppose it might be in some ghastly way. Uncle Peter falling down on his responsibilities. But not falling down any more drastically than Mum and Dad, surely? All I know is she turned up out of the blue, introduced herself, stayed a couple of weeks, was entirely charming and considerate throughout, and left. She asked me not to contact her mother and father, and I didn't. Neither Roger nor I had the slightest wish to abuse her sexually, I suppose I had better make that clear."

"Was she pregnant?"

He hesitated, before shrugging.

"Yes. She came to borrow money for an abortion. When she left, I imagine that's where she went."

"You don't know where?"

"No."

"And she hasn't been in touch since?"

"Again, no."

"But you gave her the money."

"She asked, and we gave. Cash," he added, smiling.

67

"In the summer, she went to Majorca with her mother. Did she turn up here before or after that?"

"After. She was very brown and healthy-looking, I thought."

"Okay, now listen. *Tony* gave her money for an abortion. She was to have had it in Cambridge. She was booked in, but she didn't show. Then she turns up here. And asks for the money a second time. What do you make of that?"

He was an intelligent and sensitive man. He thought for a while, his glass against his cheek.

"There are some things that can't be concealed," he said. "Like being in love, or pining for someone else. I don't think there was anyone else in the background for the time she was here. Nobody phoned her, and she hardly left the house. I had the feeling she was going it alone. And when she was ready, she left."

"Can I see the room where she slept?"

"Oh Lord," Peter protested.

"Then I'll get out of your hair."

The room was at the top of the house, up uncarpetted stairs. If I had thought of searching it, or sleuthing, as Diane's Malcolm would have put it, I was taken all sails aback. The place was a tip. At least a dozen tea chests were filled to overflowing, and on top of those were piled carpets, grubby ceiling tiles, clothes, old shoes, lengths of curtain track, tennis rackets and almost everything else these two comedians had discontinued using over the years but had been loath to throw away. Her bed was a sagging sofa jammed between all this and a wall. It could be lit from a naked 60 watt bulb overhead, and by day from a sash window repaired with Sellotape. The bedclothes, such as they were, were still on top of it.

"Nice," I said.

"There are two other rooms up here where the floor is

unsafe. We both have studies on the middle floor. This was all we could offer."

"I want to look round."

"You can't go banging about at this time of night," he said, alarmed. "Roger is probably reading."

"I want to be alone in the room for five minutes. I won't make a noise. If you want to go to bed, I can let myself out."

"I could make a pot of tea, I suppose," he muttered.

I found what I was looking for without knowing it was there. I found it almost immediately. At the head of the sofa, she had amused herself by pulling off the wallpaper and leaving behind a jagged mountain range of white backing.

Drawn in pencil on the soft, fibrous paper was a little angel with wings outstretched, wearing a halo on her head, and sporting innocent breasts with dots for nipples. She was the twin sister to the one on the wall above the Primlea Guest House. Which gave her, all things considered, a rather mocking quality. I stripped the bed and pulled it from the wall. Apart from a pair of knickers rolled into a damp rope and a peach stone covered in a winter fur coat, that was all. And heigho said Anthony Roly.

Both the other bedroom doors were locked. Well, if the floors were dodgy, they would be, wouldn't they? Waiting at the foot of the attic stairs was Peter's partner, Roger. He was wearing a huge black and white Japanese gown and had his arms folded in a posture of indignation. Though I smiled, he did nothing but scowl the harder. I had outstayed my welcome. And to be fair, it was nearly one o'clock in the morning.

Downstairs, there was no sign of Peter or a pot of tea. I left as meekly as I knew how.

Just for something to do, really, I drove into the West End and pootled round for a while. God knows what I thought I was going to find. In the end I settled for a telephone just up the street from Liberty's. Watched by two well-hard characters in an unmarked car, I got Diane out of bed and told her to leave the key in the door. Then I got back into the hire car and yawned my way into Regent St. The Christmas decorations included a little male angel blowing a trumpet. Or perhaps it was a raspberry.

SIX

The key was in the door, but there was no welcoming note propped against the tea caddy. The house was in utter darkness. I made myself a cold lamb sandwich from the fridge and drank a can of Guinness she may have intended for Malcolm. I read the obits in *The Independent* and yawned a hell of a lot. Then I stretched out in front of the fire with a chair cushion for a pillow. Apart from a taste in the mouth like old flower water and eyes itching from fatigue, things were okay. I was comfortable enough.

I dreamed I was in a restaurant with Peggy Lee, watching her sign autographs. A man at the next table was doing a paper tearing act, and he held up the zinger, a ladder of little angels. The people applauded and Miss Lee got up to sing. This was all just terrific and I was hoping against hope she would favour us with 'Is That All There Is?' when some callow person tugged me rudely by the shoulder. More, kicked me in the ribs. For a long time, I thought it was someone in the dream.

Diane's body warmed up in the mornings – I supposed every

morning – as she metabolised the booze of the night before. At eight, wakened by the radio alarm, she sat up in bed and pulled the torn nightie over her head, chucked it at the wall and crashed back beside me. Her knee parted my thighs and her head nuzzled furiously for a pillow in the crook of my arm. Her skin was slick with sweat and she burned like a barrack room stove. The image pleased me and I fell asleep again, this time dreaming of the initiative exercises at Trasfynnydd. The Army lent us the facilities in this North Wales beauty spot. It had been so cold we poor police squaddies had chopped up the War Department's chairs and lockers for fuel. There was initiative to be discovered in us once the temperature triggered it. It snowed with arctic wildness and the wind howled in the stove chimneys. The instructors had all retreated in good order to a pub at the bottom of the mountain and for two glorious days we were cut off from our chain of command. We behaved with the abandon of Serbian conscripts, stoked with British sherry and Merrydown cider. Those were the days. Don't tell me about the Cold War. I was there, kid. The Army was utterly outraged. Twenty drunken police cadets had put the whole NATO shield at risk. Eighteen chairs, folding; six wardrobes, single; and nine lockers, foot, had been consigned to the flames.

"Someone," the baby-faced Adjutant shouted in our faces, "is for the high jump."

"You are all," the Super bellowed, "a bunch of idle useless gits. Reckless, insubordinate tossers. Who have shamed your uniforms."

We woke again about eleven. I was damned pleased to get back to reality. Diane's breasts were hot against my chest. I rolled onto my back. I was surprised to find we were holding hands, like Hansel and Gretel. Little fishes danced on the ceiling, reflected from the rain puddles outside.

"Good morning," I said.

Her mouth tasted faintly of sour milk. She stroked my ribs and poked her finger in my belly button.

"How did you know the key would be in the door?" she asked.

"I didn't."

I pushed the hair from her cheek and kissed her.

"I didn't know I'd end up here, either."

"Oh, don't try to be arch. It doesn't suit you. Does this thing here do anything?"

"Only when I tell it to."

"Then tell it."

We could just about fit in the bath together, which we did while listening to the one o'clock news on Radio 4. Diane had been a bit too liberal with the salts, and a great deal of brilliant white foam was being generated. It made her skin look dark as a gypsy's. She piled a whimsical cone of bubbles on top of her head and showed me how to talk like Donald Duck. I gave her my Cary Grant. We were getting on like a house on fire. The Opposition spokesman for Trade and Industry was having to shout to get his oar in at all. Her Popeye was hilarious. When we kissed our mouths were hot with tears of laughter. The bath water crashed out over the floor in waves. Then it was as if an unseen voice had said "Now, children, don't let's get too excited." She skimmed the foam from her breasts with a forefinger and wiped her face with a flannel.

"This, I may as well tell you, is what I was born to do. That's a recent realisation. I'm enjoying it, but I don't want you to get any ideas. I'm a bit of a heartless cow, and this is just sex. Make of it what you like."

Her hands sought mine and our fingers laced.

"Sex and danger," she added as an afterthought.

"Whatever you say. But somebody should teach you to stop kidding yourself. Nothing is just sex. And you're not in any danger."

"No?" she said.

She was certainly a hedonist of real if small scale accomplishments. Soon the water was crashing over the bathroom floor again and we were having fun trying to flick the foam to the ceiling with a back scrubber. Kneeling in the bath between her legs, my cheeks skidded over slippery flesh that tasted exotically of lime and lemons. We were drenched in bubbles and laughing like hyenas. Or hysterical stoats. I wondered with the rational part of my brain how to get my life back on its tracks, if in fact it had been patiently puffing around before.

"Isn't this just terrific? And what makes it so wonderful is being told by po-faced journalists that life isn't like this. That's what makes it special."

"Where are these po-faced journalists? Send them in."

She pulled me down onto her breast with a crash of suds.

"Malcolm just hated getting his hair wet. His Barnet Fair."

"You say the most romantic things, Diane."

"It was all press-ups with him. It's great having a bag of lard like you around, with your creaking knees and your little skinny arms."

I laughed, but mainly to disguise a fit of pique.

"I mean it," she mumbled. She held me up by the scalp like John the Baptist.

After tramping down towels on the puddled floor, I went downstairs to make her coffee. When I came back up she had changed the rumpled sheets and was sitting in bed reading from her Flaubert. The radio was retuned to a concert of Byrd and Palestrina. As I came into the room her smile was sudden and radiant.

"Move in with me," she murmured. "I need someone like you. Someone daft as a brush. It can't be here much longer – I suppose he'll chuck me out soon. But we could find a place. What do you say?"

"All this? After one bath together? This is the stuff of novels, Diane."

"It would be like helping the underprivileged, if you like. And it's very definitely like no novel you'll ever read, mate. We could give it a whirl. What do you say?"

"I'm on for that. But give yourself time. Finish your Flaubert. Maybe get the Christmas shopping done. Find Melissa."

It upset her. She shrugged and looked down her nose at me.

"This is the tough guy in you talking, is it?"

"Don't you want to find her?"

"Piss off. How is Judith?"

"Judith?"

"You mentioned her in your sleep. What's *she* like in bed?"

When she saw the look in my eyes, she relented immediately and held out her arms.

"I'm sorry," she said.

"Anyone less like Judith would be hard to find."

"Is that good or bad?"

I kissed the warm silver crease between her breasts.

"Drink your coffee. Read your book. Rest your weary limbs. It's only two in the afternoon, after all, and the day is young."

"And what'll you do?"

"I'll read the paper. Then I'll wash up. Then I'll look in the coal shed and gather winter fuel. That sort of thing. But don't you get flustered. You take it slowly."

She pulled the sheets up under her armpits and poked her

tongue out at me. I went back downstairs wondering what the hell I had got myself into. A week with Diane and the world would slow to a stop. It would be twelve shopping days to Christmas for the rest of creation.

"You don't know how to relax," she shouted after me, as if I had said these words aloud.

It was weird all right. I took out the wallets of snapshots and sifted through them again, looking for Cambridge and the supper club. Tony finds his daughter is pregnant and sends her off to Cambridge, to a contact he has there. What contact? He belongs to a supper club there, but what does that mean? His own education had all the hallmarks of the University of Life Insurance – cautious, prudent, faintly preposterous and terribly, terribly dull. Apart from a goatish passion for a Filipino sex-doll, his habits are predictable.

His half brother on the other hand is living in a hell-hole in London with a man who used to be a jingle writer and wears a black and white kimono. What was it about these two Englishmen – what was it about England indeed – that made you believe that, of the two, Peter Pelling would easily grace any supper club got up for whatever purpose; whereas the more favoured brother looked like the man who might just conceivably supply the members with their wine?

I found a curious photograph I had previously overlooked. Three elderly men sat under a weeping willow, all trouser legs and white shin bones. On the ground in front of them, and to one side, was a small nylon bag with a red Canadian maple leaf stencil. Of the three, the tubby guy was the most likely to be Canadian. He was wearing one of those really expensive tweed jackets that North American thinkers wear, with an unbuttoned denim shirt. The frames to his specs were transparent and his grey hair was cut en brosse.

The man sitting next to him was Peter Pelling's partner,

Roger. I looked at the print more closely. The two men's hands were touching, maybe by design, maybe by accident. The third man was looking at Rog and the Canadian with a fine disdain, or maybe an ill-disguised envy, but that wasn't it either: what made the picture newsworthy was this stranger's tie.

You had to know this to know Diane: that while her pleasure in sex was limitless, sex was a way of running away from more mundane business. She could be extraordinarily sulky about events in the world of clocks and diaries, timetables and itineraries. Above all, she hated having to think about anything disagreeable.

"You haven't actually been listening," I complained to a shut expression. "What do you do, blank out what you don't want to think about?"

"Yes!" she snapped, defiant. "I do! That's just what I do!"

We were eating pilchards on toast in front of a sullen fire. It was by now four in the afternoon and quite dark outside. The rain had stopped, the wind had fallen, and nature was undecided about what to do next. Diane's invitation to move in was looking more and more reckless: her dismay at having to concentrate on some single topic, her evasiveness when asked to put her mind to something, was extremely irritating to me. From wrecking the bathroom joyously, we had moved to monosyllabic misery. She was drinking scotch with her pilchards.

"Look," I said. "I'll go through it again. There's a little drawing of the angel in the guest house in Hertford. There's another one in Peter Pelling's attic in Devorah St, Kentish Town. Maybe Melissa drew them both. Maybe not. And in this photograph I can't get you to look at, one of the ginks is wearing a tie with the same design on it. A tie, a club tie. Isn't that worth talking about?"

77

"Then talk about it," she said. "Talk all you want, but don't ask me what it means."

"The photograph is in your collection, Diane. You didn't take it, so that leaves Melissa or Tony. I'll take Tony. And it looks like Cambridge. Doesn't it look like Cambridge?"

"It looks like three men sitting under a tree. Okay, it's not the Sahara or Iceland, but who the hell says it was taken in Cambridge?"

She had a point. It hurt me to say so, but she had scored a hit with that one. I wanted to think it was Cambridge, for the sake of symmetry. On the other hand, she seemed to be missing the point that this was all about looking for a missing daughter.

"Tell me about the supper club."

"I don't know a damn thing about the supper club. I keep telling you that. Who is the Canadian?"

"You're asking *me*?" I shouted suddenly, outraged. "This is *your* damn photograph. It was taken on your husband's camera, and if you weren't such a complete nit we could match it to a negative. A strip of negatives. Your brother-in-law's boyfriend is holding hands with someone who might be a Canadian, in what might be Cambridge. Watched by a guy in an angel tie."

"Maybe it was taken in Canada," she muttered.

Shaking with rage, my heart fluttering, I rang the Primlea and explained I was speaking from the Department of Social Security about a claimant, a Melissa Pelling. I had her right there in the office with me, and would Mrs Gaskin just confirm that Melissa had stayed in the Guest House in the summer, she couldn't remember the exact dates.

"Who is this speaking?" La Gaskin wanted to know.

"Roy Hedges, Claims Investigation, the SS. Just have a quick shufti at your register, Mrs G, and you'll tidy up a whole mess of stuff I'm getting from this claimant."

"Nobody called Pelling stayed here in the summer," Mrs Gaskin said combatively. "Or ever. So you can tell your claimant she's lying."

"Ah," I said. "Bang goes her dosh, then."

"Good," the heartless woman said, cutting the connection.

Diane looked at me with a mouth like a coathanger, well into her third stiff whiskey.

"That was clever, was it?"

"Not *clever*," I said, exasperated. "Oh, Di, come on! Not clever. I'll ring her back in a minute and say I'm the Canadian Embassy. Or I would, if I could think of an angle."

"And then what?"

"We could drive to Cambridge."

"I'm not going to Cambridge."

That was the smart time to leave, rise, put down my pilchards on toast and bid her farewell and drive like the wind back up to the early doors at the Volunteer in Yorkshire.

Afterwards, when it was all unravelled, I wished I had. Wished it a thousand times.

Instead, I took the photograph to Pelling. He was surprised to see me, enough to sink into a chair in his study with the back of hand to his forehead like Forbes Robertson giving us his Hamlet.

"I will say this about you. You are nothing if not crude."

"I'm a lavatory brush among private investigators. The best sort, had you noticed, are to be found in crime novels. They got firsts at Oxford, are the sons of Dukes, and choose their wines with confidence. They have servants called Barnes or Noone and the police look up to them. They year is perpetually 1935. But this is now and you've got me."

"I thought the point was that I don't actually employ you any longer."

"A footling nicety. You've got me all the same. You kept your half-brother very quiet."

He grabbed at his glasses as though they were about to fly off his nose, struck by an invisible hand.

"How did you find out about *him*?"

"Melissa was there in the summer."

"No!" he cried, genuinely anguished. "Not there."

"Look, Mr Pelling. I think you're up what we in the business define as shit creek. Now I'm sure there's a very simple explanation for this. So why don't you tell me about it?"

"How do you know she was there? Did Peter tell you? It's a lie. She would never go there."

"I don't see why not."

"It isn't possible."

"Where's Pilar tonight?"

"What? In London. What's that got to do with it?"

"I think you're under the cosh in some way. I think you need to talk. Tell me about the man in the photograph, the one with the amusing tie."

"Tie?" he asked, bemused. "What tie?"

"Round his neck he's wearing a tie," I said patiently. Pelling peered at the image of the man and his tie in total confusion. He even went so far as to pick up a magnifying glass from the desk and hold it to his face, like Holmes in Baker Street.

"You've never noticed it before?"

"Never. What is it?"

"Where was the photograph taken?"

"On the Backs at Cambridge. John's, I think."

"Are they members of your club?"

"What?" squeaked Pelling, appalled at the very idea.

"The famous Cambridge supper club."

"This has nothing to do with it. Are you mad?"

80

"You mean none of these guys are members?"

"Well, of course not. Absolutely not."

"Who are they?"

"The one on the left is Bob Westerman, a Canadian. A friend. You'll probably recognise Roger Ullman. The other one was called Roskill. I'd never met him before."

"Who were you with that day, Westerman or Roger?"

"You bastard."

"Tell me."

"Bob was my friend. We met Roger and this other man by chance. We sat on the grass and talked for a few minutes."

"Where is Westerman now?"

"He's dead," Pelling said.

"What did he die of?"

Pelling looked at me with pure loathing in his eyes.

"He was murdered," he said.

Ahah. Now suddenly I'm sitting there with a picture of a man in a tie and some tomfool expression on my face and Pelling has given in and is weeping buckets. I got up and found something better to drink than his amontillado, and settled for two big belts of Black Bush, a sovereign remedy. I took them to the kitchen to find some ice. Pelling followed me.

"I know what you think," he said.

"Well, don't hold out on me. Tell me. I need to know what I think."

"You think this is something to do with homosexual practises."

I passed him his tumbler and he sat down at a chrome bar stool, wiping his eyes with a dazzling white handkerchief. The whole kitchen was no less spotless. I was beginning to regret my crack about the lavatory brush. It was a bit too close to home.

81

"Tell me," I prompted. He replaced his glasses carefully.

"It is nothing of the kind. Roger is. The man Roskill was. Probably. I am most certainly not. Not gay, I mean."

"How about Westerman?"

Pelling studied his glass, hooked the ice out of it and threw the cubes into the sink.

"I have nothing to hide. I met him in Tangiers. You can ask my former wife. Towards the end of our marriage we went our separate ways. I was in the habit of taking breaks on my own."

"Goofing off."

"If you like. I went to Tangiers and we met at the hotel. We played table-tennis."

"Oh, come on," I said, exasperated. "You can do better than that."

Pelling peered at me with his weak eyes.

"He'd picked up a girl, a young girl. She was a television researcher or something. She'd come with a friend, and the friend had gone home. Flown home. Bob picked her up. All three of us played table-tennis. We hired a car, ate out together. That sort of thing. She was a chit of a girl, not bright or anything. She may not even have been what she said she was. She worked in television, but I don't know that she was really ever up to research."

"Did she know how to use the telephone?"

"Very funny. We all three of us went to bed, that is what you are trying to find out. I paid her telephone bill and a couple of other things, small things, and the night before she left we all got into the same bed. That does happen, you know."

"And you never saw her again. But you and Bob had the beginnings of an unusual friendship going for you. I'm just trying to move the story on, Mr Pelling."

"What a revolting man you are. What sort of pleasure can you get from acting and talking like this?"

"It would give me simple and unalloyed pleasure to find your daughter for you."

Pelling hesitated. He touched the red bulb of his nose and breathed through his mouth for a moment or so.

"He was a Professor of French on a sabbatical of some kind. Back in London, we telephoned each other and I suppose I had some hope that what happened in Tangiers might happen again. It was that stupid. All this was when I was still married to Diane, of course. I am a highly-sexed man, I make no bones about it. I made none to Diane. Bob had provided a great adventure. We met a few times for dinner."

"And you took him to Cambridge."

"He went there to give a lecture, before he left. He invited me. He dined me at Caius and the next day we went for a walk. And we met Roger and this man Roskill completely by accident. It was fairly sticky. I hardly knew Roger; and Roskill not at all."

"This was *last* year, *last* summer?"

"I've told you, Diane and I were still together. Or at any rate—"

"—Yes, I know. Still married. How about your exciting and sultry housekeeper?"

"I met Pilar at Christmas," he mumbled.

We looked at each other like two people with a broken down car and ten miles to walk over the blasted heath. From his account of things, Roskill's trail was at least fifteen months old. I shrugged.

"Okay, you met them by accident. And then what?"

"We went back to tea with Sir Eric Gilderman."

"What happened to Bob?"

"I've told you."

83

"He was murdered in Canada?"

"In France."

"When was this?"

"Recently. September."

"In Paris."

"No," Pelling said. "In Angoulême."

"What happened?"

"He was found under the ramparts. He'd been mugged and then stabbed."

"Have the French found his killer?"

"I've no idea."

"What was he doing in Angoulême?"

"Again, I have no idea. Nor can I begin to see what any of this has to do with Melissa."

I told him about the ladder of angels. He listened with a jumpy, nervous intensity and the story was all new to him, of that I was pretty sure. He could see that if Melissa had scribbled the little drawing on Roger's attic wall, and Roger's chum the mysterious Roskill had a tie in the same design, we were not exactly flailing about in the complete dark; but no better than that. We had the stub of a candle, but we still hadn't found the matches.

There was a phone in the kitchen and I rang the Primlea Guest House for the second time that day.

"West Yorkshire Police, love. D.I. Cooper. Can I speak to the proprietor?"

"That's me," Mrs Gaskin said, grim.

"That's great, is that. And your name is?"

"Margaret Hilda Gaskin."

"That's Mrs Gaskin, I take it. Well, we're trying to trace the whereabouts of a Ted Gibbons. Cheque fraud. Do you have a register, do you? Could you have a glance?"

"Ted who?"

"Gibbons. Say earlier this year. You haven't had one that bounced have you? Edward Albert Gibbons. Tall guy, early sixties, bit of a plonker."

"We don't have people like that to stay here," La Gaskin snapped. "Anyway, I've looked as far back as Feb and there's no Gibbons."

"Try Witherspoon, would you? Or Roskill."

I listened to her snorting through her nose as she riffled the pages of the register.

"August 7th," she said at last.

"Witherspoon?"

"Roskill."

"Got an address?"

He had given his address as Ballycastle, Co Antrim. A thought occurred to Mrs Gaskin.

"This isn't a terrorist thing, is it? Bombs and that? My husband's not a well man."

"Nothing like that. Straight fraud. And small stuff at that. Well, you've done me proud, love, you have that."

"He didn't seem completely Irish at the time, I remember."

"The low cunning of it, eh? Is it snowing down there?"

"No. Is it in Yorkshire?"

"Can't see across the road for it."

I put down the phone and stared at a reflective looking Pelling.

"Why did he come here?" he asked.

"Exactly."

"You don't have a theory?"

"I haven't got a clue," I said, honestly enough.

"*He* could have drawn on the wall of the guest house, and he could have drawn on Peter and Roger's bedroom wall. It could all be his. I mean Melissa might be completely in the dark about him, or any of this."

"It might be complete coincidence that he came here in August," I agreed.

His look of gratitude was pathetic to behold. Though all these things might have been true, he did not think so – and neither did I. We sate in the wonderful tidy kitchen, listening to the faint clack of seconds and minutes passing across the face of a wall clock. Perhaps he was trying to remember exactly what he had said to the mysterious Roskill more than a year ago, when the four men met by accident outside John's, with the Wedding Cake and Bridge of Sighs as backdrop, and fearfully intelligent people poling about in punts.

SEVEN

Before I left a very strange thing happened. Pelling went to a desk in his study and gave me four hundred pounds in twenties, which was only as it should be; but added, with much plunging of his adam's apple, that I was in no wise to come to the house again, nor reveal to Pilar that I was still on the case.

"Does that mean that I am?" I asked, surprised.

"I should like to get to the bottom of things, yes," he mumbled into his shirt. "There have been some wild assertions made. Perhaps that's not quite the way to describe what's happened, but I am unhappy about leaving things the way they stand. All the same, I must stress: I would prefer my housekeeper was kept out of it."

It cost him dear to say this, enough to make him blush. Perhaps he already knew how much he was being manipulated by the seductive Pilar, and the price he might have paid for his other illicit adventures with the likes of Bob Westerman. In that sense, the man with the angel tie had come back to haunt him. It was last year's story, when he was trying to enjoy the fruits of this year.

"I can be as discreet as the lawn outside your window, Mr Pelling."

"I'm pleased to hear it."

And now it was my turn to blush, a little.

"I think I should tell you, your wife has very kindly offered me a room in her house," I mentioned far too casually. His eyes flashed briefly behind his fogey specs.

"I'm sure you'll be made most welcome," he said.

"And now that matter's been broached, I ought also to tell you that Pilar has offered me a thousand pounds to go away and forget I ever met any of you."

"She was, I'm sure, acting out of consideration for the family."

"I thought I should just mention that."

"Have you taken the money?"

"No."

"I am grateful to you," Pelling said, his lip trembling.

I thought of something else just as he was ushering me out of the door.

"Your dining club. Does it have a name?"

"Oh that? I don't think that comes into it. We are called the Dodos," he said. "I think you could characterise us as extreme right wing libertarians. I won't say it's harmless: put into practise our philosophies would be volcanically harmful. To certain people. Or groups of people."

"Are you planning to put this theory into practise?"

"There's no chance of that. It's just talk. It's amusement."

"Just a group of old sillies having a rant."

"Yes," Pelling said, after a pause. "Just that."

So, o.d. the Dodos and back to Diane. Diane not at home to Mr Rude. Peer through window. A big fire crackling in the hearth and a rollicking version of 'How High The Moon' on the speakers. Half a glass of wine on the littered coffee table. But no lady of the house. I banged on the front door again and stepped back to glance up at the bedroom windows. My foot crushed something soft and yet springy. I looked down, not without a touch of petulance.

I was standing on a white high heel shoe.

The ground immediately outside the house was gravelled and I got off it in a hurry. I crouched in the soaking wet shadows of a laurel and looked away from the lights to try to restore some night vision. After a moment or so, I lay full length in the pebbly herbaceous border, feeling my skin crawl vigorously and not worrying in the least about how things might look to a passing stranger. I could hear an umbrella clothes line screeching as the wind tore it round, and more distantly, a splashing noise that could be moorhens or could be something else.

At the back of the house I knew there was a dining room. She did not use it, and I had merely glanced in once. But it had French windows. I crept round the gable end, the cloth of my trousers clinging to my legs with mud and water. There were dustbins here on the side of the house: I paused for a moment.

It was actually passing through my head that I was making a meal of this when the splashing in the meadows intensified suddenly and unmistakably and became two or more people running like hell. They were maybe a hundred yards away. I jumped up and set off in pursuit, noting out of the corner of my eye that the French windows were not only open, but flat against the wall. The curtains were waving madly like prayer flags. Out in the meadows a woman was screaming.

Nobody had told me – why should they? – that Granny Pelling, who had once owned the house, favoured a string fence about three feet high to signify to nature that all on her side was private property. I connected with it going flat out and the wire caught me just below the knee. As I fell, my face was raked by some post or pole and I landed in three feet of ancient soot, hidden under a goodly crop of nettles. I floundered about in the soot, coughing and cursing, while out there in the dark the woman screamed for help. Right! Now I was good and mad and I set off down that meadow like the one and only Jonah Lumu. Up ahead, a pale figure was crossing my path. Stumbling and skidding, pumping the legs, losing a shoe of my own, but with flash recollections of being the lankiest scrum-half in the history of schools rugby, I closed in on my quarry. For all I know I was shouting *Banzai!* or *Geronimo!* into the bargain.

The little peaceable river had flooded its banks days ago and we were careering through nearly a foot of water. The figure up ahead sensed the danger in this and stopped in momentary panic. I made the hit with a furious swallow dive, shoulder just under the rump, arms encircling, teeth gritted.

Cocky Bateson, who coached the First XV, would have been proud of me. My opponent and I went under the waves together, beneath a curtain of spray.

Hit 'em hard, hit 'em low, and when they get up, hit 'em again. This was my full intention. But there were problems. First, I had tackled a half-naked woman. Second, the woman was not Diane but Melissa.

Cyril Sanderson was right: the kid had style. Wearing only a Friends of the Earth T-shirt and Marks and Sparks knickers, she pummelled merry hell out of me before I could explain who I was. Then, before we could go back to the house, she demanded – she absolutely insisted – that I find her specs, somewhere in the mud and slime.

"You stay here and look," I said, breathless. "I'm going to get whoever was chasing you."

"Don't be an idiot," Melissa said. She pointed. Just at the

edge of a long shaft of light coming from the house, a man splashed away through the water meadows. I sat down in the icy water, the foot without a shoe now also without a sock. Salty blood ran into my mouth at the corner.

"Find me specs, you pathetic nitwit," Melissa commanded.

She was fitter than I had imagined, with the same strong legs as her mother's and a swimmer's back. She wore the famous RAF greatcoat over her nakedness and held my jaw in her hand as she dabbed at the gash on my cheek with peroxide. The new logs she had thrown onto the fire hissed cheerfully. Her specs, minus one earpiece, sat comfortably on her snub nose. Despite her drenching, she smelt distantly though deliciously of lavender soap.

"You could have lost an ear, or an eye," she said.

"He jumped you outside the front door, is that right?"

"More or less."

"Was it Roskill?"

She paused for a second and looked me calmly in the eye.

"No, it wasn't."

"Who was it?"

"He didn't introduce himself. He was going for me and I ran."

"Going for you – what with? An axe? A rolled up copy of the *London Review Of Books*? A sixteenth century Florentine dagger?"

"I rang the doorbell and he came out with his hands round my neck."

"Didn't you have a coat? Or a bag?"

"Out there somewhere."

"How about your skirt?"

"He pulled that off in the fight."

"Just a passing skirt-snatcher, was he?"

"I don't know who he was. A yob."

"You didn't recognise him?"

"Oh, sod off," the former student of European History and one-time Shakespearean actress said.

"Where's your mum?"

"Not here. Evidently. Perhaps you'll get tetanus. If you do, you'll die in agony."

"How about pneumonia?"

But before she could answer, I pushed her over and straddled her waist. She – understandably enough – put a poor construction on this and we fought for control of her arms. Moreover, she was trying to throw her legs up behind my back and tear my head off in the crook of her knees. She hadn't been wasting her time since running away from home: someone, or some way of life, had taught her not to mess about with niceties when straddled by dirty old men. She was out to kill me.

But I was not out to rape her. I had seen something when she was dabbing at the cut. I managed to force back one arm flat to the carpet and with the palm of my other hand – her fingers in my eyes – I pushed her firm girl's breast to one side.

High up, under the muscle and just below the armpit, was a tiny tattoo. When she saw that I had seen it, she ceased altogether to fight. She lay on her back panting and glaring at me through her owlish glasses. I pulled the greatcoat over to cover her chest.

"You're heavy," she said, neutral.

I rolled off her. Blood was running down my throat from where she had smacked me in the teeth. More blood from the cut on my cheek dropped horribly onto the carpet.

"Who did it?"

"Did what?"

"Tattooed the angel on you."

"Mind your own business. And clean yourself up."

She pushed on my chest with strong arms and stood up for a moment before sinking down into her mother's chair.

"How much do you know?" she asked.

"Sweet F.A. is the answer to that."

She laughed and then put her head down on her knees with a howl. I staggered to my feet and went into the kitchen to put the kettle on. Uppermost in my mind was her father, sitting in his immaculate house only a few miles away, trying to convince himself that none of this sudden storm of shit descending on him had anything to do with his daughter.

"What happened to the baby?"

"What do you think?"

"Come on, don't cry. I don't want to give you a bad time – I'm supposed to be here to help."

"That's what they all say just before they take away your benefits."

"Really?"

"I don't want your rotten help."

On the draining board, I found a page torn from an exercise book, a note addressed to me from Mum. I was a real bastard and she must have been mad to put me up for the night. She had left the spare key in the door so that I could pick up my bits and pieces and clear out for good. She was going out for a drink with Malcolm and sucks boo to the lot of you. I read this tender message and chucked it in the trash. It explained how Melissa's attacker got into the house – but who was he waiting for, mother or daughter?

"This is tea I'm making," I called. "Milk? Sugar?"

"Are you one of Mum's lovers?"

"Nothing as grand as that."

"What are you doing here, then?"

"Your Dad hired me to find you."

"I bet."

93

"Come on, Melissa. Head up, be a man about it. They were worried for you. Tell me about the tattoo."

"Oh, I would do that, wouldn't I?" she scoffed.

"I hope so, yes. The bloke that was lying in wait for you here wasn't too friendly. And you were running for your damn life. Six months ago you were trying to bone up on Bismarck and wondering whether fat people should wear horizontal stripes. Now you've got a tattoo you might not always want and some bozo trying to kill you."

"Not *kill* me," she scoffed.

"What else? He wasn't trying to get your autograph."

I passed her a mug of tea with milk and no sugar and chucked a log on the fire. She had hung her T-shirt and bra over the fireguard: the fabric was hot and moist. She snatched the shirt out of my hand to wipe her eyes.

"Well say something, you nit."

"You look terrible," she said. "And you smell."

"You look terrific."

"I've never met anyone as corny as you. What a jerk."

"This is my gentle side you're seeing. My caring aspect."

"I'm going to have a bath," she said, jumping up and tramping out of the room on sturdy legs.

I riffled through Diane's CDs and found, to my genuine delight, fifteen tracks of Nancy Wilson in a mellow mood. When I was sure Melissa was actually taking a bath, I went upstairs and found a T-shirt of her mother's and a pair of Malcolm's jeans I had noticed hanging behind the bedroom door. I carried my own reeking clothes downstairs again and chucked the lot in the washing machine. Then I washed my battered face under the tap, while Miss Wilson explained how yesterday's kisses were still on her lips. Soot was running out of my hair like Indian ink.

She, too, raided Diane's wardrobe. She came down wearing a baggy pink blouse and white cotton harem trousers. Her feet were bare. Her hair was wet. There was enough resemblance to her mother to cause me covert anxiety. Melissa laughed.

"You look awfully funny. Uncle Peter told me to expect a bit of a clown."

"Uncle Peter is a pain in the bum."

"No, he's not," Melissa said. "He's sweet. Who's this singing?"

"Nancy Wilson."

"Crap," she decided. "If you have got tetanus from that cut, you'll be really ill. You ought to get it seen to. Have you seen my father recently?"

"Earlier this evening."

"And he fed you a lot of lies, no doubt."

"I didn't get that feeling, no."

"Well, you can't be very perceptive."

"Where are you living these days?"

"Oh, you know, London, Paris, New York. That sort of thing."

"And you thought you'd call in and see your mother on one of your lightning visits?"

"Peter told me about you. I came to find out more."

"Well, here I am."

She smiled. That much at least had happened to her since she ran away – the expression was much more mobile. Smiles, frowns, laughter, irritation chased each other across her face: somewhere or other she had grown a lot in confidence. I watched her half whimsically tweaking up the material of her harem trousers, already a lifetime away from the stolid presence she had offered to the punters who frequented the *Blue Skies* studios down the road in Broxbourne. She looked up at me with a frankness that was almost startling.

95

"I'm okay," she said at last. "You can tell them that, make them see. I'm clean, I'm not doing any drugs, and I'm making some serious money. Nobody's using me. It's true I have a tattoo on my breast, but that's all. Nothing more terrible than that. When I'm ready, I'll make contact in the proper way. But when *I* decide. Tell them that."

"They think you may be in danger."

"No," she retorted. "*You* do. *You* think I'm in danger. But the only threatening person in my life is you. I'm coping. Better than that, I'm getting somewhere. Doing something. I really came to warn you to mind your own business. I can't stand busy-bodies."

"What about the man who chased you into the meadows?"

"Is that minding your own business?"

I had spread Tony Pelling's twenty pound notes out to dry, and she turned them over, like toast.

"I'm not often warned off by a teenager in specs," I said.

"Don't be a jerk. I know people who will blind you or tie your hand to an electric stove for less money than this. You thought you were looking for an overweight schoolgirl with soup for brains. That's all over, that part of my life."

"Tell me about these people that you know."

"Don't make me laugh," she said.

I was, to put it mildly, losing the initiative. And to be sure, when she looked at me, her glance was not that of a girl, but a woman's; calm, poised.

"Who got you pregnant, Melissa?"

It was intended as a shock question, but the answer floored me by the speed at which it came back.

"Cuddly Bob Westerman. Didn't Daddy tell you?"

Her story began with Westerman coming to the house the previous year, while the family was still together and Pilar was

96

yet to appear on the scene. Pelling introduced him as a new friend. He was on his way from the Bibliotheque Nationale back home to Toronto. It was summer. He called by chance, flustering Tony, but stayed for a barbecue. Melissa was working upstairs on her homework. He called up to see her and stayed a few minutes. He sat on the end of the bed and teased her about being a swot. She found him merry and bright, with a breath of something romantic about him – Paris, perhaps. He gave her some book titles of things she should read and described his own work briefly. Leaning over her desk, he put his hand on her shoulder.

"He was very calm and polite on the outside. But I knew there was something there, something in it for him. I don't know how I knew, but I knew."

Downstairs, Tony Pelling was furiously fighting charcoal with lighter fuel and Diane was uncorking (out of pure spite) her husband's jealously kept Pomerol. When Westerman was called, Melissa turned her head for a polite goodbye. He kissed her on the forehead for just a fraction too long. She thought him a bit weird. He was giving off signals she had never before received from a man.

"That was last year," she said. "He went home and sent me a necklace and an Esquimaux carving. His letter was a bit iffy, but I was a kid, of course. He seemed very fond of Daddy and they wrote to each other a lot. He phoned up. That sort of thing."

"Then your Mum quit and Pilar appeared."

"Yes."

"When he phoned, did he ever ask to speak to you?"

"No. He asked after me."

"Did you write to him?"

"I'd more or less forgotten him. He was right. I was a great swot."

Something occurred to me that I had yet to ask her parents.

97

"How did you do, by the way?"

"Three A's," Melissa said negligently.

In early July of the following year – the year we were in now – she had been alone in the house when Westerman rang from London. He was passing through on his way to Paris. The Canadian chatted amiably for a few minutes and the astounded her by asking her out to a meal. He meant in the West End. Flustered, she put him off by saying, truthfully, that she was going to a concert in St Albans. At six that night he turned up in a hire car.

"To take you to the concert."

"He's a very cultured man," she said, bitter.

But there had been no bitterness that night, or not to begin with. Melissa was an honest witness, no matter what it cost her. She sat in Diane's chair, drinking her mother's Vin D'Alsace telling me about something terrible that had happened only six months earlier, and speaking like a woman. She still looked like a schoolgirl, or at any rate a student. But the girl who had gone to St Albans with Westerman would never come back.

She had been astonished by the strength of her feelings. Westerman was the first man to have paid her the slightest attention. He was in fact her first date. She talked too much, drank too much in the pub afterwards. She was flirting with his mind. On the way back, Westerman turned off the road and drove until he found a wooded area.

"And raped you."

"Felt me up to begin with. But then, as he said afterwards, he couldn't stop himself."

"What happened? Did you fight him?"

"Yes."

"And he hurt you?"

"Getting a thrill yourself now, are you?"

"Look at me, Melissa," I said sharply.

She glanced into my eyes briefly and then shrugged.

"Yes, he hurt me. If it happened now, it would be very different. But I was an idiot then."

"You didn't tell anyone what happened?"

"The doctor down the road. Who's in his sixties. He thought it was all very shocking. Needing stitches, and so on."

"Stitches."

"Yes," she said, with a level stare.

"You didn't tell your parents?"

"He was my father's friend, remember?"

"Your mother? Pilar?"

"Grow up," Melissa said. "I let a man in a car take me to a wood and rape and bugger me. And do anything else he liked. Because I was pissed on three glasses of Pernod and a brandy. Because I thought he was interested in what I had to say about Louis XIV. And because when it started I couldn't believe it was happening."

"Then what? Did you see him again?"

"No," she said, dreamily. She gazed into the fire for a while. I bit the inside of my lip, trying to answer a question in my head.

"You never heard from him again," I said carefully.

"There were no more Esquimaux carvings, no."

She toasted me across the rim of her wine glass with a faintly mocking air that I found completely chilling. Now that I had found her there was plenty to baffle me about her. She watched me thinking this and smiled. In her new vocabulary of facial expressions, this short smile of hers was creepy beyond belief."

"You'd like Mummy to come home and get you out of this, wouldn't you?"

"How about I make us both a vegetable curry?"

99

"Terrific," she said, and switched on the television.

There was a lot to think about. It was true: I would have liked Diane to come home. It was gone ten, and getting towards that witching hour when Hertford loses its public transport and becomes unavailable for anything short of the impact of giant meteorites. Melissa lolled in the chair, her legs hooked over the arm, watching George Segal and blowing raspberries. But we – and perhaps Diane and big Malcolm – were the exceptional couples. Everywhere else, commuters were getting their clothes ready for the morning and wondering why the hell they were paying a mortgage for a place they only used for five waking hours a day.

"This guy that attacked you. I don't suppose he was a big bloke, over six feet tall, a squaddie sort of character?" I asked, in a fit of sudden inspiration. She was impressed.

"How did you work that one out, Holmes?"

I was thinking of Leslie's bonehead brother in the Dragoon Guards. It was the sort of frightener he might dream up. But then people who put the frighteners on other people *are* big as a general rule. You don't get five foot two fiddle players from the LSO moonlighting in that area.

"Did he say anything?"

Melissa laughed.

"I did ask for his name and address, yes. He was very sweet about not giving it."

"And you're extra cool."

"You should meet some of the people I know," she bragged.

"Oh yes?"

The curry was going well, by my own modest standards. I opened another Vin D'Alsace and she came out to join me in the kitchen. Enormous changes had been wrought to her in a few brief months.

"Was the baby aborted?" I asked.

"Don't call it a baby. It was his prick, him, that I was getting rid of. And let me tell you something: I don't spend days or even hours thinking about it. Any of it. It hasn't wounded me. I'm a whole person."

"Have I said anything different?"

"Old people have these ideas," she muttered darkly.

"Want to tell me what you're doing nowadays?"

"Fuck off," she said, cheerfully enough.

We ate on our knees in the living room. She talked a lot. We got on, as they say, like a house on fire. We discussed the kind of music she liked (none, was the answer to that one); about the politics of poverty; London; and her mother. She could do a very good imitation of Diane. From somewhere or other she had picked up a rich new confidence, which included facing down an attacker in a flooded field: but there was a residue of Melissa the lonely one, the child upstairs rattling her pen in the bottle of Quink and thinking about Bismarck reading telegrams and eating arrowroot biscuits. When she jumped up to make coffee, it was my chance to turn off the television. Staley was back on the ropes and his Lonsdale Belt was going out the window. He looked towards his corner and then looked at me, his gumshield hanging out of his mouth. Do something, his eyes said, before his picture faded to a white dot.

"Uncle Peter says you don't like the human race very much," she called from the kitchen.

"That's a bit rich, coming from him."

"Rubbish. You don't know the first thing about him."

"There are two things to know?"

"What an old fraud you are. Has Mummy got you into bed yet?"

"A disgusting question."

"You're her type. Scruffy."

"My best quality."

"I'm flirting with you, a bit."

"Oh yes?"

"I only really do it with older men."

"Do me a favour, Melissa. Stop bragging."

"I'm telling you the truth."

"We needn't talk about it."

"I like talking about it."

"Okay," I said. "Did Roskill tattoo your tit?"

She was on her way in with the coffee. She set the cups down without the slightest sign of being fazed by the question.

"Who's Roskill?"

"Does he tattoo all his little chums?"

For a moment she seemed merely perplexed, but then a vast irritation seemed to overtake her.

"God," she said. "I thought you were clever. But you don't know anything at all really, do you? Stand up a minute. I want to show you something."

I stood. Before I could say Robert Robinson the sole of her bare foot hit me in the stomach with a punch like a mule's, and I fell to the woodsmoke-smelling carpet, my chest heaving for breath, my legs scrabbling.

When I got to my knees and cleared the tears from my eyes, she was gone. So was Tony Pelling's four hundred, and so were the keys to the car. I staggered to the door and saw the tail-lights bouncing away into the night as the moon flew like an owl through the scudding clouds. Without regrets, I said goodbye to the curry I had just eaten right there on the steps of the cottage.

Here is a girl who in a few months has learned how to drive a car, curse like a bricklayer, fell a grown man with a single kick. She's had an abortion, been tattooed, most recently been attacked in the dark by someone trying to shove her head under the waves. She's lost a stone in weight, had her hair cut, taken up the mini-skirt: by her own account, she runs with a wild bunch who can take all this in their stride. She's making good money and generally coming on strong. In London, presumably. We don't know who she's hanging out with, but they're not likely to be mewling and indecisive under-achievers. Mixing with them has made the Roman in Melissa into a Grade A Goth.

Diane came home at midnight. She'd had a bad time, too. Malcolm had got the lady next door to baby-sit while he took her to the Green Man, a pub so remote from street lighting and roads with real pavements as to be safe from prying eyes. Unfortunately for them both, Cyril Sanderson had booked Malcolm's missus to do a mid-week Yuletide gig at this very same pub. The sultry songthrush had finished her set, and then, before Diane could run and hide, walked over and poured Malcolm's Bass over his head. In the ladies, she had pushed Diane's head down into a basin and broken her specs. It was all very embarrassing. She'd had no help at all from the craven Mal and was forced to spend a fortune coming home by cab. When I told her she had missed Melissa by no more than an hour, she threw her handbag at the wall and wailed.

EIGHT

This time I did sleep downstairs. Diane went to bed with the last of the brandy and locked herself in. During the night a few flakes of snow fell, lending the cottage a romantic air it had otherwise mislaid in the past few days. I huddled in the all purpose RAF greatcoat and found it very useful at first light, when, wearing a huge pair of wellies I found in the garage and sporting a rake, I set off towards the river. After an hour and a half of sloshing about, working in a box pattern to be sure, but with dewdrops as big as golf balls on the tip of my nose, I came in for a cup of coffee. To my surprise, Diane was already up. She even looked contrite. She took my frozen hands and tucked them under her armpits, and kissed me on my unfeeling lips. Without her specs or eye make-up she had a peering, uncertain quality. Tears glistened in her eyes.

"Don't be ratty with me," she mumbled.

She made me coffee and told me all about the unhappy Malcolm, who had submitted to being beaten up by his platinum blonde witch of a wife like a hapless goof. It seemed that not only did big Mal have beer poured over his head, but the lapels to his Next jacket had been torn off and his face spat upon.

"Then, she follows me into the loo and tries to stuff my head down the wash basin plug hole. That woman is demented. I mean she is walking about showing just as much bosom as a cow in milk, half wearing a really horrible mauve sheath dress – with sequins – and singing stuff like 'Cry me a River'. She's terrible! Just awful! And then she comes over to beat the daylights out of one of the punters. It was terrifying. People thought it was part of her act. They thought it was funny."

"She loves him," I suggested.

"Oh, don't be so wet."

She stared gloomily out on the upturned rake, with the waves crashing around it.

"What are you doing out there?"

"Looking for Melissa's bag."

"Brilliant!" Diane cried. "Absolutely bloody brilliant!"

So out I went again, this time with her half-finished tam over my ears and a tonic bottle of hot whisky, orange juice and demerara sugar to keep me alive. Diane stood at the bedroom windows, blowing me kisses.

As I raked, like some figure in a Kurosawa movie, I pondered. The tattoo linked Melissa to Roskill. Roskill wears his angel on his tie – Melissa's is under her armpit. They are at the very least in the same neck of the woods. Roskill – I raked away vigorously at this one – Roskill is in Hertford a day or so after Westerman's second visit. Was he invited? Did Melissa call him up? Was the nasty end to Westerman in any was a consequence?

However it was, the Canadian, who should today be safely chasing skirt in Toronto and shopping for his Christmas presents, is buried in a foreign field. On the other hand, Melissa seems to think he's still alive. That doesn't quite fit.

And then there's the problem of Melissa's startling transformation from frumpy swot to karate queen. How does that fit?

When I was playing house with Tania in lovable old Yorkshire, she came home one day with fifty business cards she had printed on the station. They read: * *Patrick Ganley* * *Private Investigator* * *23 3/4 hour service* * In Tania's undemanding world, this was a funny – and because funny, memorable – sort of business introduction. We even sent a few out. Tania had never fallen foul of the law and knew no one who had been seriously damaged by crime. Crime was something that happened in the newspapers, or was reconstructed by actor-extras on public service slots late at night on regional television. The world was an unceasing glut of little events – Owen's goal, Baker's haircut, Sean's movie, Julie's by-pass operation, Kosovo's agony. The world was like the weather: changeable, but at the same time, dependable. Essentially, the world was about forgetting. Once in a while I would take her old newspapers out of the cupboard and run them to the tip. They would thud down on tons of newsprint, millions of dead words. What was mint in Tania's life was what was happening tomorrow. By eleven most mornings, even today was dead.

And accordingly, she disparaged the kind of work I did. For someone like Tania, who killed Bob Westerman was none of my business. What Melissa was up to was even less of my business. It was all out there somewhere, bowling along like tumbling tumbleweed and about as interesting. I was a fool to take it any more seriously than, say, the Indonesian elections, or the price of a set of pegs and a clothesline in old Bombay. It was strictly a waste of time. You can't really live your life like that, but you can make a good pretence of it.

I found her skirt at half past nine. It was hardly more than a provocative fifteen inches long – was Little Miss Brainbox

106

really walking about London in a mini, bare legs and white high heels? I read the label on the skirt and chucked it back. I was fishing for bigger game. It began to snow again. Just when my feet had lost all sensation and I was ready to wait for spring, the tines of the rake snagged on the strap to a satchel bag. I hauled it up, threw down the rake and stumbled back through the snow. The house was almost invisible. I staggered round to the front and found Diane cleaning up the kitchen and listening to Hadyn. I stood there on the threshold looking like Worzel Gummidge. She threw her arms round my neck.

"You're gorgeous," she said. "You're wonderful! I'm not going to let you go until you promise to stay for Christmas. I've got it all planned out."

"I'll be in hospital over Christmas. You can reach me in Intensive Care."

She flew upstairs and ran me a bath There were no regular bath salts left, but she raced into the bedroom and found four grubby little silver balls of essence that had been rolling around in a drawer for a year – since last Christmas, in fact. She wanted to look in Melissa's bag straight away, but I had done all the hard work and I was in no mood to be tampered with. I shooed her from the bathroom, chucked the bag down in a squelching heap, got into the bath and fell fast asleep, wrapped in the fragrance of water the colour of pink flamingos. At midday she came up with a further whisky toddy and kisses for my eyelids. She washed my hair for me and we went to the bedroom, me to sleep some more and she to read her Flaubert. I was a real dynamo in the run-up to that Christmas, no doubt about it. Diane later said she preferred men who knew their own weaknesses. She woke me up about three, when the sky outside was the colour of anthracite. I was childishly pleased to see her.

"Go on, open the bag," she whispered after a while. "Bring

107

it in here and let's peek. It was fiendishly clever of you to think of looking for it, and just brilliant of you to find it."

"You're a nice woman, Diane," I said. "I mean it. But maybe I should just make you a present of the bag and leave."

"Leave?" she cried, alarmed. Considering she was straddling my chest and had just been amusing us both by dipping her breasts into my eyes, it must have seemed a bit of a daft thing to say.

"I don't know what we'll find. Her address, maybe. Her new identity. Enough, anyway, for you to trace her, if you want to. But maybe a whole lot more that you wouldn't be too happy about."

"Rubbish. You don't really want to leave, do you?"

With her, everyone was safe if they stayed in bed and made love as often as possible. It was not easy to get her to see that opening Melissa's bag might be like incoming mortar fire in the middle of an orgasm.

"I've found out how she got pregnant and who made her pregnant," I said by way of an experiment.

Her face crumpled immediately. Her lower lip jutted.

"I don't want to talk about it," she said.

"That's *it*. That's my point. I mean the bag might just contain her address or some current ID, or it might have more things in it you don't want to talk about. And then what? That's my damn *point*. What you don't want to talk about makes a pretty long list!"

"Bastard!"

"I found the bag out in the meadows, you daft bitch, because someone was trying to kill her out there. Drown her, shove her head underwater. Try and get your mind round that one."

"Don't shout. And try not to call any woman a bitch. It demeans you, as well as half the human race."

108

"Di," I pleaded. "Try to think for a moment."

"I am."

She pouted and made faces and lifted herself from my chest. She put her head in my hands. I realised that all this time the clock radio had been playing very quietly. It was by now almost dark. Alarmingly white snow hurled itself at the black window panes. She snapped on the bedside light.

"Okay. It could be bad. And I suppose I have to find out. I've got to, I suppose. But you could help. You could put everything right. We could do it together."

I reached and kissed her plump, rounded shoulder.

"Three days ago you didn't know I existed."

"What in heaven has that got to do with it? That seems a completely illogical statement. You're here now, aren't you?"

"Last night—" I began patiently.

"I was angry with you last night, yes. But today it's different."

She rolled away and turned her back, narked. There was a large mole on her shoulder blade and faintly watery layers of fat creeping round her ribs. Her back shook.

"I'm crying," she wailed.

So I went to the bathroom, emptied the bag of rain, pulled on Malcolm's jeans, still soaking wet at the cuff, and carried the loot downstairs. I shoved it next to the fire while I made some tea. Diane appeared in a sweater and jeans. Her voice was small.

"I understand what you're saying. And I really and truly don't want you to go. I'm stupid, I know that too. I'm crazy about you. That's the most stupid thing of all to have happened. But what can I do on my own? Have a heart, Patrick. You can help me fix it all up. Please."

I gave her a mug of tea and played with the logs in the hearth for a while, trying to get the smoke to go up the chimney,

109

and not rush back down into the open room when it felt the breath of winter. She lit a lamp. She went upstairs and found a baggy sweater. It smelt of her moisturising cream. I spread some back copies of *The Independent* to act as blotting paper.

"I trust you," she said weakly, meaning I can't think any more, I can't act for myself. She reached for my hand and held it for a moment or two.

I opened the bag and tipped the contents onto the newspaper spread between our feet.

She was still Melissa Pelling. She had an address – Wendell Street. Diane looked it up in a dog-eared London A-Z she pulled from the bookshelves. It was off the Uxbridge Road. It seemed to fill her with delight – she pictured villas that had become maisonettes, arty people, BBC folk. She saw lovely Indian people staying open all hours to sell fresh cardamom and inexpensive plonk to bright young men with pony-tails.

We discovered that Melissa combed her hair with a fierce looking Boots brush, possibly while chomping Polo mints, of which there were several packs. She blew her nose on loose white tissues and applied lip salve from time to time from a green dispenser without its cap. Inside a box of matches was a little silver ball with a little pellet of dope – but no skins. She may have had some call on the services of G.V. Godley, Plastering Contractor, whose card she had; or broken bread at Stuffie's, of Covent Garden who gave out purple books of matches. There were till receipts from the Co-op, local tobacconists, Waterstones, two or three garages, half a dozen other places. I set the garage ones aside.

There was a used return ferry ticket from Stranraer to Larne: she had travelled on it as a foot passenger in early September. There was a sheet of strawberry pink writing paper bearing the words – not in her handwriting – 'Left at x-roads, continue on, Ch at 1. very small road off r., 2nd house

110

on l. Love Ernest.' There were two condoms taken from a pub vending machine; a white postcard with a Brighton telephone number on it; a flier about a new restaurant in Shepherd's Bush with a six digit number scrawled across it, but no code; and a creased photo of Diane. There was a single drop earring repaired with fuse wire, and cash totalling two hundred and twenty seven pounds 53p.

As all these things were laid out clockwise on the sheets of *The Independent*, Diane returned every few seconds to peering in the pages of the A-Z, breaking off for a fond chuckle now and then.

"There you are!" she said triumphantly. "Nothing nasty about any of that. Just a normal working girl's handbag."

I sipped my tea.

There was no cheque book, nothing from a benefits office, nothing at all to suggest employment or unemployment, no diary, and above all, no keys. The cosy little flat Diane was picturing for her was suggested by an address scrawled across an empty envelope. The stamp had been cancelled in Cambridge on November 12th.

"Perhaps the keys were in her coat. Or perhaps they fell out of the bag in some way."

I walked to the cluttered baby grand and by dint of shoving stuff round, found the phone. I rang the Brighton number and got a polite and querulous old man.

"Hallo," I said, "just checking: should Melissa be with you again this week?"

"Melissa?" the voice warbled, incredulous.

"Mmm. A perfect little angel."

The line went dead.

I held the phone out to Diane.

"Ring him back, say you're the supervisor, ask him whether he's been getting nuisance calls lately. And get his name."

111

But she could not or would not do it. Instead, she seemed to cower. I dialled 192.

"Directory Enquiries, which town please?"

"Ballycastle, Northern Ireland."

"And the subscriber's name?"

"C.V. Roskill."

There was a pause.

"There's nothing listed."

"Is there not one in the book?

"I'm sorry, caller," the stolid, weary voice murmured.

I glanced back at the fireside where Diane was slumped.

"This is it," I said. "You can send a Christmas card to Wendell Street and leave it like that. Maybe she lives there, maybe she doesn't. If she ever turns up here again, you can remember not to ask her about going to Northern Ireland or any of the rest of it. She's a big girl and she knows how to look after herself – I'll vouch for that. She can kill a mule with those happy feet of hers. Some joker has tattooed her tit, but perhaps that's just lurv. There's a lot more, Diane, but I don't want to get pissy with you."

"Say it all, why don't you?"

"She doesn't have a licence or own a car, but has kept receipts for petrol from Kent, Sussex and Oxfordshire. For someone who's nineteen she's carrying a lot of dough. She's mixed up in some way with this gink Roskill, who's a pal of someone you know called Roger. I don't like the sound of Roskill. But then – as people have often said of me – I don't like anyone very much."

"Finished?"

"Almost. Your daughter came here last night. She came to see you. Not Daddy Pelling, but you. There's half a million hanging about in a safe somewhere for her to collect and she doesn't make a beeline for Dad and sweet-talk him into hand-

112

ing it over with some yarn of training to be a cocoa analyst with a firm of City stockbrokers and a boyfriend called Jeremy and where's the cheque – she comes out here to talk to you. As herself. Who she is, now. And waiting for her is someone we know nothing about who – at the very least – intends to scare her shitless. She's not my daughter and you're not my wife. But I think we should do something."

"We could go to Wendell Street and if she's all right, if she's happy—"

The phone rang. I expected it to be Melissa in some irrational part of my mind, but it was Pilar.

Diane seemed to have forgotten that her car was where she left it the night before and mine had been stolen by Melissa. While we sat waiting for the cab to arrive, Diane held the empty Wendell Street envelope to her chest, as though it could explain everything. And I, old misery-guts, held Melissa's readies to the fire to dry them sufficiently to stuff in the back of Malcolm's jeans.

"I think I warned you," Pilar said. "You are messing me about and I don't like it."

"You're looking pretty good tonight, Pilar. How was London?"

In fact she looked gorgeous in a black silk shirt and jeans. We sat in what she must have chosen with care as being the least fashionable and thus from her point of view the safest pub in Hertford. My gumboots, about which I had some misgivings before setting out, did not raise an eyebrow. About thirty low-lifes were downing the A.K. as though tomorrow the brewery would run dry. Frank Sinatra was commanding us all to have ourselves a Merry, Merry Christmas. A tinsel Christmas tree with a broken plastic foot leaned morosely against the bar and the Alsatian had eaten all the crepe paper

113

streamers he could reach. There were a few cards tacked to the wall, most notably one of a big girl leaning out of Santa's sledge and giving us our Yuletide cleavage.

"I don't know how to get it across to you, but I find you very unfunny. Nobody is doing anything wrong. We're just ordinary people with ordinary family problems. And yet you will keep stirring it for everybody."

"What's produced this little outburst?"

"The police have been round this evening."

"Oh really?"

"Yes, oh really," she snapped. "Peter Pelling has been murdered."

I stared at her incredulously.

"Where was this?"

"On Hampstead Heath."

"When?"

"Last night. He was beaten to death. Anthony is dreadfully upset. He was found today, this morning."

I walked to the bar and ordered two more. The boys were talking about whether any player – *any* player – was worth eight million quid. The explosive Emmett, a twenty-two year old kid from South Shields, had just been transferred to Arsenal. I thought of the good natured and tolerant old man with the Audenesque swish of hair, face down in the snow. She watched me carry the drinks back with a frowning expression.

"Has there been an arrest?"

"Of course not."

"What about Roger?"

"You think Roger killed him?" she scoffed.

"You give me your candidate."

Pilar banged her little gold lighter on the table with impatience.

"That's it, that's what I'm talking about. I'm Tony's

housekeeper. All right, I didn't grow up in a convent, and I've done things in the past I'd rather forget, but I've nothing to do with any of the family except him. You understand? Can you get that through your skull? I'm just his housekeeper."

"Then why don't you mind your own business?"

A small stand-off. She turned the lighter over and over in her hands. Somehow or other, it *was* her business.

"I've worked hard to get where I am now," she muttered absently.

"The police think he was rolled for his money?" I suggested.

She hesitated.

"He has been in trouble with the police in the past. A long time ago. But it seems incredible he should be out there at his age, I mean with his years."

"You talk as though you know him."

"That's because I do know him. I met him before I met Tony."

Was she being careless and was I hearing something that really mattered? I sipped my beer trying to imagine under what circumstances Pilar and the genially impoverished Peter might meet. It seemed the most unlikely chance encounter, unless she ran him over on the way to the off-license. But what was I going to do – bash her head on the table until she spilt the beans?

"What is Tony doing about it?"

"He's gone to see Roger. Who's tried to slash his wrists. It's a mess. We were supposed to be going to the Bahamas for Christmas. Listen. I'm going to tell you just enough for you to get off my back. All I want out of this is what I've got. Understand? If you keep on hounding me, I'll have you stopped. Look at the guy in the leather jacket at the bar. Drinking vodka and tonic."

I looked.

"What about him?"

"I want you to talk to him," she said; and pushing back her chair, left.

He was called Denzil and reminded me vaguely of show business people. Under his leather jacket he wore a pink cotton shirt with a button down collar. His jeans were crisp and fresh. Denzil had seen his fortieth birthday some time ago and his heavy head was almost bald. But he was a serious guy all right, with his pale eyes and Spanish tan. Practically the first thing he asked me was where I was going for Christmas. He was off to play golf in Florida.

"This isn't your speed round here is it? Listening to these tosspots talk about Emmett? It's a joke. You probably seen the boy at Elland Road, when he played Leeds. He's magic."

"Pilar said you had something to tell me. Not about football."

Denzil nodded calmly.

"That's it. She said you were a piece of shit. I don't rile easily. Try to understand what I'm saying. I've got as much sense of humour as the next guy, so if you do say anything funny, I'll laugh. But you don't impress me as a comedian, not as a hard man. So don't let's arse about."

He told his story easily and with perfect casual emphasis. I suppose he paid me the flattery of assuming I knew the score so far as people like him were concerned – he was not some knuckle Pilar had called up from the back room of some pub. He was modest about it, but Denzil was a heavy duty guy. He got me to see that in less than three minutes.

"I do favours for people, Mr Ganley. I'm well known for it. For friends, of course, and for people of importance, top people, you might say. I assist in their immediate problems in

116

areas outside their competence. The rest of the time, like I say, I'm just Mr Nobody, Mr Goodnatured Chump. Play off six, mind. I hold the course record at Cobb Creek. That's in Philly, as I expect you know."

It had already crossed my mind that he might have been the one who spent last night wrestling with Melissa in the flooded field.

"What'd you drive?" I asked idly.

"A Porsche. Pilar was right about you. You're a bit of a joke, Mr Ganley."

"What sort of golf clubs do you use?"

"Ping."

"Patek watch?"

Denzil merely smiled.

"Pilar's a personal friend, is she?"

"That's what I'm here to tell you, chump."

Pilar came to Europe when she was eighteen on her passport and thirteen in fact. She came as the wife of a third officer on a Bremen tanker. This man, who was still her legal husband, looked after her for almost a year in his home town of Bodhum and after teaching her as much English as he knew himself, brought her to England. They stayed in London for a week while certain negotiations took place with an Arab millionaire through his intermediaries. Then the German said goodbye and Pilar went to live in the Arab's mansion in Holland Park.

She was seen out very seldom, except with an Englishwoman called Fay, who more or less ran the household and kept things happy. Denzil had met her at parties held in the house – the crack I'd made about sport had been an ill-judged one because he was an Olympic judo medallist turned bodyguard.

"Not for the gentleman who had this place in Holland

117

Park, for someone else. But I saw her a few times. She asked if she could go to Goodwood – he had horses running there – and I took her. We met one of the Royals, that sort of thing. Then I went to the States – to Hollywood – for some other business for a year or so. I kept in touch, sent cards and that. Fay let me know how things were going on. She was doing very well."

When she was actually eighteen, the millionaire bought her a little house in Fulham and made her a present of money, enough to live on if she was very careful. But as Denzil explained, she soon made some choice mistakes. He lived with her himself for a few months until they quarrelled. She made contact with the German again, who was by now bigamously married to another sporty type, a shot-putter. He got her a job in Dusseldorf. Denzil came over and rescued her from that: they lost touch again. Then he heard she was working in the hotel business. After nearly two years she met Tony Pelling and that was that.

"That's the story?"

"That's what she wanted me to tell you," Denzil corrected in his even, unhurried way. "I've never met Mr Pelling but I understand he's a nice man, a decent sort. And she's happy. Or she was, until you turned up. And that's the story. Understand what I'm saying?"

"You'd like me to lay off."

"She's just a nice kid who doesn't need grief. I like her. I admire her. That's enough, isn't it?"

"I'm looking for Pelling's daughter."

"She told me that. She also told me she offered you money to piss off. I'm what you might call the next stage. Understand what I'm saying?"

"You're the muscle."

Denzil studied his glass, frowning faintly.

"I've got a friend, an actor, good actor. I mean someone bankable," he explained. "He had a little problem the other side of the Atlantic, a little unpleasantness he couldn't sort out for himself. I was in Turkey, on holiday as it happened. He managed to find me, I flew to L.A., rented a car and sorted it out for him. For good. The boy – it was a rent boy with no sense, no style – was out of order. So I offed him. It sounds shit, but it's what happened. And now here I am, talking to you."

"Would you off me?"

"What we're talking about is someone we both know who wants to live a nice quiet life. I've explained all this. She wants to marry this Mr Pelling and no problems. That's the sheet on this one. But to answer your question, I'd tear your head off just for the exercise," Denzil said, patting me affectionately on the arm.

"Ever met the daughter, Melissa?"

Denzil sighed.

"You're thick as pig shit, Mr Ganley. You just don't listen."

"No, no, I've heard every word you said," I gabbled hastily. He wasn't the one who attacked Melissa at Goose Cottage, I was sure of it. I was absolutely sure of it. Sometimes you just *knew* about these things. Denzil studied me with his pale blue eyes. At last a faint smile came to his lips.

"Good boy," he said.

NINE

Just to keep things tidy, next morning I got Diane to phone Malcolm. The poor guy was hiding under the desk in his office and had to be coaxed to meet me. We chose a café in Ware, found the pubs were open and changed our minds.

"Bloody hell," Malcolm said fervently. "It don't matter that this gink Sanderson is slipping *her* one. That's never going to come out, or if it does her rotten parents will probably say it's the show business. Look, tell Di I'm really sorry, will you?"

"She's being philosophical about it."

"Yeah, good. But tell her to lay off. No more phone calls. I nearly crapped myself this morning."

"Is your brother-in-law home on leave?"

"Yeah," he said wonderingly. "What the bloody hell happened? He came home soaked to the skin. You didn't do him over, did you? He's supposed to be a trained killer."

"He met his match," I said, not without a little dishonest preening. "Listen, I've got to go, Mal. But just one other thing. When you were doing the work in Kentish Town – the place you saw Melissa last year – did you meet an Irishman? A bloke from Ulster?"

"He was a friend of theirs," he said instantly.

"Was he a friend of Melissa's?"

"How the hell should I know? He was all right."

I stood and drank off the last of the pint.

"Look after yourself, kid. Love to Leslie. She's probably planning a wonderful Christmas for you with all the trimmings."

"My balls nailed to the front door with a sprig of holly," he agreed gloomily.

Across the road from Peter Pelling's house in Devorah Street was a corner café. Maybe it had once seen prosperous times, but not any longer. There were five tables covered in scuffed and torn red American cloth and a tea bar with the fascia kicked out. Lighting was from four ceiling spots, only three of which worked, and the wood round the windows was black and rotted. There was a faintly sickly smell cutting the fug of the place, a smell sharper than the stuff coming off the empty griddle. There were two posters pasted to the wall – one of Brando in *The Wild Ones*, and the other of a nun adjusting her stockings.

A young couple with a baby ran this place, and they looked just about beaten by the challenge. She was one of those over-bright, over-enthusiastic kids who has probably dreamed the idea up in the first place, of taking a little business and being one's own boss. She was very pale and thin, with a long nose and bony wrists. Every once in a while she took the baby out of its buggy and went behind the counter to feed it at the breast. Her incessant bright smile and rainbow clothes were perhaps a form of hysteria. The husband was stockier, more phlegmatic. He did what he could. But you just felt awful watching the three of them, because *The Peppercorn*, which is what they called the place, was never going to make it. They were called Julia and Lawrence, and the baby was called Penn.

"Of course," Julia said, after the first few hours, "we don't really believe you're waiting for someone. And it does matter. See, Lawrence had some money from an Industrial Tribunal and this place is all we've got."

"What are you trying to say, Julia?"

"We don't want to ask you to leave, you know, make a big number of it, but you could see it from our point of view, perhaps."

"I could order something else to eat," I said, "but why don't I just give you the money for the food and ask you not to bring it to the table?"

"It's just that we don't want to get mixed up in anything. What with Penn and everything. If you look at it from that point of view."

The heating was provided by a paraffin stove. It convected the brown slush tramped in by the occasional customer but did nothing to warm the room evenly. Condensation streamed down the windows nearest the stove. I had seen Roger come home by hospital cab, his wrists bandaged, and watched him walk indoors. I could even see the naked bulb hanging from the ceiling rose in the front room, where Peter Pelling had talked to me.

"You're not mixed up in anything," I said to Julia. "I have to wait for a man, that's all."

"Yes, but you see we don't really believe you. I shouldn't say that, use those words, but you know what I mean."

I ordered an all-day breakfast for £3.45, and asked her not to cook it. The husband was standing at the grill with his arms folded, his expression anxious. He wanted her to get through the day without dismay. He believed in her, was her dogged foot-soldier and trusty lieutenant rolled into one.

Julia went out a little later with the baby. Lawrence came and sat with me, smoking an illicit roll-up, his head in his hands. Julia was the kind that goes forward to give the tank commander a flower in hope of appealing to his humanity.

Lawrence was more sanguine. We talked about football. He had once played in goal for a parks team in which all the outfield players were black, with the exception of a Greek schoolboy who went on to play for Crystal Palace. That was his big number, knowing Connie Lefkadis.

"Julia's a dreamer," he said with a slow smile. "She thinks everything can be lovely if only people are nice to each other. And that people will be nice to each other as soon as everything's lovely."

"You're a lucky guy."

"Yes," he said. "You don't believe that."

"Not quite in the same way as Julia, no."

"So who is this bloke you're waiting for?"

"I'm watching that house across the street, Lawrence," I said gently. "It's a job, the job I do. As you probably guessed."

He glanced.

"The Old Bill were there again this morning. Took away some stuff in plastic bags. We never got them in here, I mean the man who was murdered and his friend. They used to drink down the road, that's all I know. Are you Press?"

I showed him the photograph of Melissa taken with her mother in the Majorca nightclub. He nodded.

"She stayed for a few days in the summer. She came in here and asked us for a job. Can you believe that?"

He laughed, this big, good-natured boy who doted on his wife and child.

"There's all kinds of shit going down in this neighbourhood. All over London, of course. But not in here. I stay awake at nights thinking about that. We don't attract

123

anything. We're living on pennies and daydreams. We're too small to be turned over, even. We're just nothing."

He smoothed away crumbs from the table with the palm of his hand.

"Like it's my birthday, right? Julia sent me to watch Palace play at Loftus Road. I got out the Tube at White City, and just... I don't know... had a fag and came home again. I couldn't bring myself to spend the money. And she cried."

"Did your pal, the Greek kid, score?"

"Twice."

Across the road, a cab drew up and the man called Roskill got out. From a distance he looked like a provincial school teacher, fussy, bad-tempered and faintly out of his depth. It took him forever to pay off the cab and one reason was that in his arms he carried an enormous teddy bear, sheathed in polythene. Roger had come to the door of the house and was waiting for him. He had yet to take off his shapeless and ancient tweed overcoat. His bandages peeped out like the cuffs to a shirt. When the cab pulled away, the two men stood staring at each a moment, before Roger turned and Roskill tramped up five steps after him. The door closed.

"And now what?" Lawrence asked.

"I don't know," I said, dispirited.

"Isn't he the one you've been waiting for?"

"Yes, maybe – I don't know."

It was the teddy bear that had thrown me. If it were a present for Roger, it spoke about him in a way I wasn't quite ready to face. I hesitated another few minutes before taking out a hundred in twenties and scribbling Diane's telephone number on the top one.

"I want you to go on watching the place opposite for me. You can do that without a hassle from anyone. Who goes in, who goes out. You don't even have to tell Julia. When you've got anything to tell me, ring that number."

"I don't know," Lawrence said, uneasy. I pushed the money to his side of the table. He looked at me for a moment or two before folding the twenties carefully and shoving them into the patch pocket of his market-bought polo shirt.

"How do you know I won't chisel you?"

"It's in your eyes," I said.

The address in Wendell Street had one thing going for it. Inside a mesh compound was my hire car, spattered with mud and slush, badly dented in one wing, but comfortingly mine. I rattled the padlocked gate to the property, watched by a fat-boy skinhead looking through a ground floor window.

It was not a house at all in the usual sense of the word. My guess was that it had once been a dairy depot or something of the kind. It was crammed between the unsightly backside of a corner shop and the first of a row of boarded up villas. This was Rat Alley we were in here. It was true that less than a hundred yards away, in the spirit of London housing, there commenced properties that did have bay trees in tubs, and black Venetian blinds. But this end of Wendell Street was a different story.

The fat boy stared at me rattling his cage for him. I pointed to the car and then to the first floor. I did this with great vigour for a minute, until his eyes at last got through a message to his brain and he lumbered out. Though it was bitterly cold, he was dressed for a midsummer barbecue in jeans and white T-shirt. He was fat, all right: but he was also plenty muscled. Flakes of snow danced on his shaven head.

"Yeh?"

"I want to see Melissa."

"Yeh?"

"So open the sodding gate."

"Wha'?"

125

"Open the gate."

"Nah."

"Open it."

"Jus' tolja. Nah."

"Look sunshine, I'm Roy Steffens, right? West Central CID, right? I've got a court order to serve on your girl Melissa, understand what I'm saying? You are impeding the course of justice. Got that? Now you open the gate, or I call a couple of vans and make big trouble for you. Right?"

"Yor Roy oo?" this kid said, maddeningly.

"Just open the bloody gate."

Melissa appeared in the doorway behind him.

"Open the gate, Wayne," she said, as if speaking to a dog. Wayne turned back to face her. This was new input. He cocked his head on one side, as if to make room.

"You want me to open the gate?"

"Yes," Melissa said.

"You sure?" Wayne asked.

I gave her back her bag in a stuffy and narrow little room that had been painted yellow by hands now long since ash and bone. Melissa took it without checking the contents and passed me the keys to the rental. She sat behind a rickety desk, and I perched on a huge and cold radiator.

"What goes on in here? Are you melting down gold fillings into ingots? Or is it a secret government research lab?"

"Wayne's only doing his job," she said.

"It isn't much, but he does it very well. So what is this place?"

"A recording studio," she said, after a pause. "And other things. Did you find your shoes?"

I showed her my grey plastic numbers, purchased in Hertford that morning.

126

"Terrible."

"You stole my car and my money. I was strapped for cash."

Artless girl, without checking her bag she opened a drawer and gave me three hundred back of what her father had given me. I was ahead in this part of the game.

"Your ma would like to see you, Melissa. She missed you by that much. She wants you to go there for Christmas."

"Will you be there?"

"Probably not. There's something else. Peter Pelling was rolled on Hampstead Heath a couple of nights ago."

"Is he all right?"

"No," I said gently.

"Where is he, where can I see him?"

"He's dead," I murmured.

The phone rang. She picked it up, listened, said yes a couple of times, and replaced the receiver.

"Do the police know who did it?"

"No. Or not yet."

"I want you to go. Leave. I mean now."

"I've only just got here."

Melissa pushed her chair with a screech on the chipped tiles and stood.

"Wayne's security, of course," she said. "When I call him, he'll chuck you out, no questions asked. And don't say you're not afraid of him, he'll break your back."

"I am afraid of him. Are you having a staff party here at Christmas? Don't give Wayne too many bamboo shoots. And the moment his eyes go the slightest bit red, make your excuses and leave."

"Goodbye, Mr Ganley."

"What time do you finish? I'll buy you a drink."

All this in a building that was eerily quiet. We had walked up worn stone steps to get to Melissa's office, and the big thing

127

about the place, its significant feature, was a new steel door at the end of the corridor, a door with a combination lock. What was going on behind it? Were old age pensioners making paper roses?

"What's your position with this establishment, Mels?"

"We make people happy here. We couldn't make you happy – nothing could please you. But there's absolutely nothing illegal about what we do and the money is excellent. Tell my mother that."

"What's behind the door?"

"What door?"

"Now you're talking like Wayne. The big steel door out there in the corridor."

Wayne would have torn my arm off, probably, but she was not long since a sixth former with a passion for truth. She pushed past me and I followed her into the corridor. She punched four numbers and there was a small click as the lock sprung. She opened the door and ushered me in.

I had half expected drugs. The room was long and lofty, with steel A frames supporting a roof of greeny-black fanlights. In front of us were three parallel benches of telephones and tape recorders, maybe as many as forty. The incoming calls were indicated by winking lamps. A skinny kid with cans on his head wandered round, sampling. Melissa passed me some headphones and plugged me into the nearest recorder.

Mandy and Sue were two wet girls living in a spanker's playground. They were just ordinary girls who liked to be slapped and slippered, but one night when they were well juiced they'd got mixed up with these right horny blokes and—

I unplugged the jack and walked down the aisle between the equipment. The skinny technician glanced at Melissa, who waved him away. I chose another recording at random. This time the voice was her's. Maybe the script was, too. I felt my eyes stinging a little. I pulled off the cans and flung them down on the bench. Melissa was watching me with guarded defiance.

"This is better than reading History at Oxford, is it?"

"Yes," she said.

"What about the booths at the end?"

She glanced.

"We have three interactive lines, obviously."

"What does that mean?"

"You ring us. We give you a confidential number on a recorded message, you ring back. We talk to you live."

"Is that the company 'we' or does it mean you when the occasion demands it?"

"I started with that side of it," she admitted. "I manage it now. I'm the manager. So what?"

"So what? You have half a million from your gran on deposit, is so what. You have a mother and father who love you. I know it's tough being a poor little rich kid, but this is sick. Who owns this dump – Roskill?"

"I don't know what you're talking about. You asked to see in here and you've seen. So now buzz off."

When we got back out in the corridor, Wayne was waiting with a black girl huddled into a woebegone fake fur. She was so cold her skin was turning yellow. Her legs were bare and she wore open toe shoes covered in brown ice. She was perhaps seventeen years old.

"'s Lelia," Wayne said.

"Wait in my office, Lelia," Melissa said. "I won't keep you a minute. Can you read, by the way?"

Lelia nodded uncertainly.

"There's a mag on my desk. Pick something from it. I'm going to want to hear you read. I'll bring you down some coffee. Open the gate, Wayne. Mr Ganley's taking the car that's in the yard."

He lumbered away downstairs. Melissa waited for me to follow him, her expression still defiant.

"Tell me the truth, Melissa. This is Roskill's business, isn't it? He owns it."

"Yes," she said, after a pause.

"And he got you into it."

"I asked him for a job."

"Oh come on," I shouted, making the stairwell ring.

"Why are you so angry?"

"Because you can do better with your life. This isn't making people happy. This is ripping off unhappy people, and in the process exploiting and debasing women. You, that kid in your office, all the others that work here. And all women generally. It may be legal – just – but it's just stinking up the world some more."

"What do you care?" she shouted back.

"Your father's friend Bob Westerman isn't in Canada. He's dead. He was murdered. Your uncle was murdered. Somebody tried to murder you. And you're mixed up with a turd like Roskill. That's enough to be going on with."

"It's a job," she bellowed. "A job. Some old drunk that goes round cadging beds and meals, and you think you can lecture me? You! You don't know anything about anything!"

The black girl, Lelia, peeped out of Melissa's office at us, her face anxious and alarmed. Melissa waved her back inside with a furious gesture.

"The only thing I am exploiting is the stupidity and greed of men. Got that? That's what this place is. And that's all it is. And it suits me fine. So now get out."

"Bob Westerman was murdered," I repeated, as patiently as I could.

"Good! Brilliant! He deserved it."

And she meant it.

She was young enough to have an unlined face and the eyes of an angel, but just then her expression was twisted with hatred. I began downstairs just as Wayne was coming up to get me. I waggled the car keys in his face and pushed past him, smelling his deodorant mixed with freezing cold air.

TEN

The snow that was being churned up on the roadways lay still and reproachful in the fields – except for those around Diane's place, which were flooded with black and racing water, reflecting back the car headlights. The track had disappeared, and I inched along, navigating by the lights of the cottage. All this weather was a boon for local radio: the first white Christmas for seventeen years was forecast, and Chris and Mark, Dave and Simon, Wendy, Sharmia and Caitlin, after a calendar year of laughing like drains at their own jokes, actually had something to broadcast – or something they could understand: "Well, Mark, the thing about driving in snow is…", or "Yo, Kringle people! Here's a goodie for you: students at West Herts Coll of E are building the world's biggest snowman … there's a mug 'n' a T-shirt for the listener who rings in with a name for the snowman. Ring now, on…"

Diane was listening to Schwarzkopf. I don't know whether that wasn't even more depressing. I made myself coffee and went upstairs for a shower. She followed me and sat on the floor of the bathroom, drinking Bourgogne.

"You found her," she said.

"It shows in my face, does it?"

"She rang me."

"Fine."

"How is she?"

"Didn't she tell you? She's just terrific."

We were both heading for a show-down, and we both knew it. I used every little bottle of gunk I could find and showered and lathered like a porn star. I had the feeling that I might not be staying in drowned and freezing Hertford much longer. Nor did I want to quit the shower and face Diane. After a moment or two, she wandered out, as far as the bedroom. There was a television in there and she watched Channel 4 News with the volume at the max. I dressed and went downstairs. Brandy was wrong: there was no whisky. I poured myself an Absolut vodka and filled the glass with ice.

They'd asked me to find their kid and I had done just that. I'd found out a lot more. The verb was far too generous – a lot more had been scuffed up in the search. But so what? Was I being paid to hunt down crime like the caped crusader? This was about me now and what I wanted. I needed some space round me. I needed at least two fillings in my teeth. I needed to stop smoking and use the money saved to work out at some health club. More urgently yet, I needed to put down the vodka, find the keys to the car, and blow. Instead, I fell asleep in the chair for a few minutes, my face reddened by the fire, my dreams flitting like a pigeon tumbling through the air. When I woke, Diane was sitting on the floor, staring into the flames. The room was eerily quiet after all the television racket.

"Tell me what you found out," she said, dull.

"She works at this place in Wendell Street. Off the Goldhawk Road. I don't know where she lives – I didn't stay to find out. But it won't be difficult to discover. You or your

133

husband could always reach her there at work. She seems to be in charge there. I guess she goes there most days. From the receipts she had in her bag, I'd say she lives locally."

"Good," Diane said, with dangerous calm.

"Well, that's it."

"Good."

"Give me a break, Di. She has a job which this man Roskill gave her. It's legal, more or less. She's not doing drugs or sleeping rough, she looks clean and fit. The job stinks like something on your shoe, but so do a lot of jobs nowadays, I suppose."

"Like yours, for example."

"Yes, like mine. Nobody asked me to save her soul, just to track her down. And there she is, okay? She has plenty of untaxed money to throw about, she carries condoms in her purse, she eats out in Covent Garden—" I thought of something else suddenly – "she's wearing contact lenses ... and she says she'll get in touch when she's ready."

"And now I'd like you to tell me all the rest. All the little bits you haven't yet bothered me with."

I hesitated.

"Isn't that for you to find out by asking her?"

"You think I'm acting sour, don't you Ganley? I *am* acting sour. Presumably you'll go back to Tony and collect the last of your money and then head off back to Yorkshire or wherever. Mission accomplished. In time – say in a week – you'll forget all about us. Someone will give you a job tracing a bad debt and you'll go and screw up someone else's life."

"What's brought this on?"

"Tony rang this afternoon to tell me that Peter Pelling has been murdered. Which, apparently, you knew all about. I'm supposed to play the fat cow who finds out everything last of all, am I? Well, it's not going to be like that any longer. I want to know everything you know. I want his money's worth out of you before you do a bunk."

I reached and took her hands in mine.

"We don't have to talk like this."

She knocked the gesture away.

"We don't have to pretend either."

I told her everything I knew. She wept a lot, but silently. It was a hard story to tell. In the end it was a three vodka story. Diane was hearing things she may have already guessed at – I don't mean about her daughter, but about life, the corkscrew nature of other people, the worm that's always in the bud. She wept and she listened. I tried very hard to make it all as dispassionate as I knew how.

Melissa is made pregnant by the Canadian, Westerman. Shortly after that, Roskill turns up at the Primlea Guest House. Shortly after that, Westerman, who should be studying archives in Paris, is found murdered in Angoulême.

"Okay, stop there. What do you mean, Roskill turns up in Hertford?"

"Yes, I've been thinking about that. It's as though he came in response to a call. But who called him? Melissa? Your husband? I don't think she asked him to come. This is July of this year, remember. Melissa was all A-Levels and concert-going – or she was until Westerman got to her. She was a shy, brainy girl with a teddy and a pot of pencils for company up in the attic. I don't see how she could have known someone like Roskill before she left home. Not enough to bring him to Hertford. Does it seem possible to you?

"Tony, then."

"Maybe. But wouldn't Tony have had him up to the house? You don't phone someone up for help and then book him a room in a cheap guest-house. We know from the photo-

135

graph taken in Cambridge that they met the previous year.
Tony says briefly. Maybe, maybe not. But however slender the
acquaintance, wouldn't Roskill have been invited straight to
the house? Isn't that what Tony would have done?"

She studied her wine.

"Yes."

"You were still living there when they first met, remember.
Did he ever mention Roskill? Did you see any unusual letters
– from Northern Ireland, that sort of thing?"

"No."

"Maybe he phoned the house? I'm guessing, but let's say
he has an Ulster accent."

"No," Diane said. "Nothing like that."

"Well, that's what happened. Westerman makes her pregnant, and Roskill appears soon after at the boarding house. It
can't have been coincidence. My theory is that somebody
asked him."

"How about Pilar?" Diane asked.

We gazed at each other, while the logs crackled in the grate
and the wind howled in the chimney.

"It's possible," I said finally.

"You don't sound too enthusiastic."

"Roskill doesn't seem her speed."

"She's a whore, isn't she?" Diane asked brutally. "And
Roskill's in the sex business."

I looked at her very sharply.

"I didn't say what business he was in."

It was a bad mistake that she'd made, and her face showed
it. She slopped some more wine in her glass. She tried to blus-
ter it out, even so far as to stand and walk to the hi-fi for some
music.

"Just a minute, Diane. This is important. How did you
know what Roskill does to make a living?"

"You must have told me. Suggested it, anyway, by the way you spoke of him. I got that impression from what you were saying."

I shook my head.

"Try again."

"Go to hell," she said. "Melissa told me."

"I don't think so. How about making it you who called up Roskill this summer?"

"Me? How the hell am I supposed to know him?"

I thought about it. She was right: it seemed almost impossible. I turned it all over in my head, fuddled from the vodka. Roskill turns up. He has business in Hertford. He can drive back into London in an hour, but instead he stays the night in a guest house. His visit is secret. He phones someone from the Primlea. While he talks, he doodles a little pubescent angel. Melissa has a secret. She has a terrible story to tell, which won't be revealed until she goes on holiday with her mother and breaks down at the airport. Pilar has the odd secret of her own, but Tony and Diane Pelling seem as guileless as china cats. She watched me, her mouth and eyes ugly.

"It was Melissa who got him to come, wasn't it?"

"It looks that way."

I told her about the little ladder of angels, the last of which I had uncovered in that very room, tattooed on Melissa's breast. I reminded her of the ferry ticket from Stranraer to Larne, and the Ballycastle address.

"But I can't remember the date of the outward journey," I admitted.

"How did she ever come to meet a shit like that?"

One answer was through the now-dead Uncle Peter. I had this flash recollection of Roskill earlier in the day, getting out of the cab and toting his enormous teddy bear up the five steps to the house in Kentish Town. The incongruity of the burden he was bearing began to sink in, a little. How do you console a man who has just lost his long time partner? By buying him a giant teddy bear? Was that Roskill's idea of a healing gesture? It was both intimate and sinister, that damn toy in its polythene sheet. It made the house in Devorah Street seem a very weird place indeed.

"I want it all explained." said Diane in a flat tone.

"It's all over. There isn't anymore."

"I'm really not stupid, Patrick."

I put my arm round her plump shoulder and after a minute she turned her face to me and buried it in my chest. I stroked her hair gently.

"You should stop now. Your daughter may be mixed up in some way or another with a murder. The trouble about finding out how and why in things like this is always that the more you explain, the more you need to explain. Westerman may have been killed for his wallet, or because he said the wrong thing to a couple of hard-cases on the ramparts, or any of a dozen reasons that lead back to Melissa."

"You mean revenge."

"It is just possible. I don't think you want to know how she came to meet Roskill or any of that. I think you should let sleeping dogs lie. Both of you – you and Tony."

"Sleeping dogs!" she exclaimed. "That gets you off the hook very neatly. But what about a ticking bomb?"

I thought about it, while she cried and the logs crackled and the reflection of the flames danced in our drinks. For a family of jaw-cracking ordinariness, as they had once been, they had certainly made a mess of this particular Christmas.

We ate. She was very tense. Our conversation teetered at new levels of politeness and civility that were only making things ten times worse. She asked me about my marriage and the

138

career I'd thrown away in the police, and what the police thought about me now. The answer to that one was easy enough: I was just another civilian. I had not seen or spoken to anyone I knew who was still a serving police officer for two years. This wasn't quite true – I had actually met someone I knew on the Met in a restaurant about a year ago. His wife talked to me hurriedly after he had cut me stone dead. We hid behind the coats while I waited for my bill. The man, who had once been a great personal friend, read the menu with deep attention. When his wife rejoined him, he did not look up.

"What did you feel about that?" Diane asked.

"Sad," I said, after a long pause.

"Do you have any friends left from that time?"

"Nope."

"Do you ever try to make new friends?"

"I get on well with people in pubs. I always nod to neighbours."

"And you are, of course, incurably facetious. Or do you call it a talent to amuse?"

"I'm a solitary, Diane. That's the same as being a loser. A lot of people end up that way, married or not. Some don't. They retire and play golf, or have the regulars in stitches down at the pub. But a lot do."

"And what makes you like it?"

"An inability to overcome circumstance. Some people are there to eat the world – Pilar would be an example. Whatever's put in their way, they just gobble it up and spit out the bits they don't like. I think your daughter may be the same."

"Am I?"

"No," I said kindly. "You're like me. You get disappointed."

"Not quite in the same way as you I don't. It's coming out

139

of you like a bad smell. Your star signs must be terrible."

"It's Neptune with me. I'm being followed around by a planet. It's personal."

When the phone rang, she answered, before holding it out to me. It was Lawrence from the Peppercorn Café. His voice was so quiet as to be almost inaudible.

"What am I supposed to be doing to earn this money?" he asked.

"Relax. Can you talk? Where's Julia?"

"In bed," he said, after a pause.

"Did you tell her anything? Can you talk now?"

"No. And yes."

"The man we saw get out of the cab. What time did he leave?"

"He's still there, or he was an hour or so ago."

"Lights on downstairs, that sort of thing?"

"Yes. A woman came with a girl at about six."

The hair on my arm rustled.

"How old was the girl?"

"Fifteen?"

"And what time did they leave?"

"The woman left by cab just now."

"And the girl?"

There was a long silence from Lawrence.

"Look," he said at last. "You saw how we're placed, the kind of people we are. I can't do this sort of thing. I won't be able to keep it from Julia and I don't want her upset. You better have your money back."

"Don't be a fool, Lawrence. Just another couple of questions. The woman and the girl. Did they know the place – did they walk up without hesitation?"

"They had a piece of paper in their hand," he said miserably.

140

"Have you ever seen that happen before? Girls coming to the house?"

"I told you: about the one who asked us for a job."

"Were there others? Before? Since?"

This time the silence at the other end of the phone was so long that it was an even more eloquent answer to my questions.

"Don't worry," I said. "Keep the dosh. I may have to call in to see you, but it'll just be for a cup of tea. Just like any other punter. You're out of it. Look after yourself, Lawrence. Give my love to Julia and Penn."

Diane was watching me as I sat down again. I rubbed my hands together in a sort of washing gesture, something I had spent my adult life trying to cure without success. She waited. There was a huge unspoken demand in the air and so in the end I told her all about Lawrence and Julia and how I'd seen Roskill go into the house opposite with his teddy bear. I told her about the girl who was there now, even as we talked, with paperbacks on the fire for fuel and the smell of dry-rot on the stairs.

"Oh Christ," Diane sobbed.

In the morning, I typed a report on everything I had discovered and Diane took it into her husband's office. The temperature had dropped and the fields round the cottage were iced over. According to the local news, vandals had destroyed the College of Education snowman in the night. A Hertford man had been killed on the A10 in a twenty car pile up. A Mrs Wall of Bengeo was just back from visiting her son on the Falklands and had seen flying saucers circling. Caitlin had some Christmas party tips on her lunchtime show and there was a mug 'n' a T-shirt for the best poem about office parties. It didn't have to rhyme.

The sky had cleared and there was a glitteringly crisp horizon. I used her vacuum cleaner on the sitting room and cleaned the kitchen from top to bottom. I went outside and checked the oil for the central heating, chucked salt over the flags that led to the house and shook the snow and ice out of some of her shrubs. When the car returned, I saw she had someone with her. It was Tony Pelling.

He looked grey in the face and ready to burst into tears.

"I asked Diane to bring me over here," he said. "You'll understand there are parts of your report that ... that are very upsetting to read."

His voice trailed off. I felt a huge wave of sympathy for them both. He absolutely amazed me by asking for a cigarette. When it was lit, he sat on the edge of an armchair, still in his topcoat, his hands shaking slightly.

"We cannot agree what to do."

"It seems easy enough. I would satisfy myself that Melissa is perfectly okay in the short term. Which I think she is. Then maybe you could talk to her about what you want, or what you hope for in the longer view, and leave it at that."

"You don't understand."

"He has something to tell you," Diane said.

I cocked my head at Pelling, not without feeling a sinking of the stomach. His adam's apple sawed up and down furiously.

"I was there when Westerman was killed," he said at last.

My jaw sagged.

"You saw him killed?"

"No, of course not. I was there in France. We have a place there," he mumbled.

"You have a what?"

"A place, a house. It's very small. A cottage, I suppose. Near Angoulême."

I turned to Diane.

"You kept that very quiet."

Pelling shook his head vigorously.

"Diane knew nothing about it. I bought it for Pilar. She wanted it."

"Marvellous," I said. "So you and Westerman thought you'd shoot over for a bit of a bash, did you? He'd just raped your daughter, but that wasn't going to stand in the way of things."

"Leave him alone," Diane said sharply. "He didn't know that at the time."

"Or did he?" I asked. Pelling fluttered his bony hands at me.

"You think *I* killed him?"

"Did you tell Pilar where you were going?"

"Yes," he said after a hesitation. "I had a practical reason for nipping over there. I'd contracted a builder to make some alterations. She knew, yes."

"Did she know you were going with Westerman?"

He hesitated again.

"Yes."

"And how about Melissa – did she know?"

He looked at Diane, who shrugged. Pelling looked at me with pure misery in his expression. His voice sank to a whisper.

"I suggested the three of us went, Westerman by train from Paris after he'd finished his business there. Melissa and I by car."

People in this business say some incredible things. You can't insure yourself against it. I felt a huge punch in my heart as fear released buckets of adrenalin into my system. I stared at him in amazement.

"Wait a minute. You suggested to Melissa that she go to France with you. To see dear old Dr Westerman. Who you

143

had yet to discover had recently raped and buggered her. And she *agreed*?"

"She was in a strange mood," he said, with the understatement of the century. "She was very difficult about it. But yes, she agreed."

"Why?"

He peered at me over his half moon glasses.

"I'm sorry?"

"Why did she agree?"

"I don't know," Pelling muttered.

"Well, have an intelligent guess. Was it to forgive him for what he'd done? Was it to ask for more of the same once the stitches were out, because though it hurt like hell, it was really a lot of fun?"

"She was pregnant by him," Diane snapped.

"I know. I just want this clown to work it out. I want someone to start thinking in your bloody family. What was *your* reason for wanting to see him?"

"Friendship," Pelling muttered, almost inaudibly.

"Say again? Did you say friendship?"

"I thought of him as a friend," Pelling shouted, spit flying from his mouth. He wiped his lips with the back of his hand. "I didn't know about all the rest of it."

"That's better! Losing your rag is better! Because what you're telling me is dynamite, enough to blow you both to kingdom come."

"I thought Melissa would welcome the break. I was happy to have found her something to do. You sicken me, Ganley. What I did was in perfect innocence."

"The point is that they went," Diane said. "That's the point."

"You're not kidding."

"Cut that out," Diane snapped. "Westerman was

144

supposed to join them and didn't. They stayed a few days and came home."

"That's exactly how it was," Pelling said.

"You said you were there when he was killed. You mean the day he was killed."

"I was forty kilometres away."

"With Melissa."

"Yes, with Melissa. We drove to Angoulême to meet the night train from Paris. He wasn't on it. He had an address and our telephone number. We went back to the cottage – the house – and waited a couple of days. He didn't show up. I know why now, of course."

I jumped up, my feet sliding about on the little hill of papers and unopened bills by the side of Diane's chair. Her tam o'shanter was to foot, and I kicked it the length of the room. Husband and estranged wife looked at me with real alarm. Pelling's alarm I could deal with, but Diane's made me want to tear the wallpaper off the walls with exasperation.

"It's a lovely story. It's an everyday story of really dopey folk. And it'll read well in the French papers. But what the bloody hell are you telling me for?"

"Because we don't know what to do," Diane said.

"During the time you were there, was Melissa ever alone?"

"I had to go into town to see the builders, yes."

"And did she ever go out alone?"

"By bicycle, yes. She went for rides. It's right on the Charente, this place."

"For how long? She went out cycling for how long?"

"In the afternoons. I can't remember the exact times. Why are you asking these questions?"

"Did you kill Westerman, Mr Pelling?"

"Good God, of course not. Why should I?"

"Exactly. You didn't have a reason. At the time you were

145

so appallingly ignorant of your daughter's welfare that you didn't have a motive. Westerman was your friend."

"You surely don't think Melissa did it?"

"I looked not at him but Diane, whose expression was so grim and guarded, so defensive, I wanted to kick her after her tam o'shanter. Our eyes locked. I had recently made love to this woman, entered her, belonged, been admitted; and our eyes examined each other now with a coldness far more gripping than the ice on the fields outside.

"I think you should talk to a solicitor," I said. "I think you should cancel Christmas. I think I should leave you to it. In fact, let's be definite about that. I'm out."

"You bastard," Diane said. "I hope you rot in hell."

"Maybe. But let's take a little bet. All this will go under the carpet with the rest of the junk. You were absolutely right to point out that I don't have any children. But I know enough about your damn child to give me nightmares. How much more is there to know? To find that out, you'd have to talk to her. But that wouldn't be your way. Maybe it'll all go away, Diane. Maybe Father Christmas is listening to us right now in Toyland and tugging thoughtfully on his beard. Maybe he's got a good idea. But not me. I'm out."

She walked up to me and hit me as hard as she knew how with the flat of her hand. I asked for it, and made no effort to defend myself, but the sting made my eyes water. I tasted blood in my mouth.

"Who do you think you are?" she asked, through white lips. "You talk a lot, but all that interests you is money. And you're cheap. You call us irresponsible, but what's so fucking wonderful about being Patrick Ganley? You're running away from life all the time. You're just another rat in the maze. And now get out of my house."

146

ELEVEN

I left Hertford that afternoon the way I had come, by train. I rang Tania in Yorkshire from Hertford North BR and she hesitated only a little before saying yes, come ahead. There was an hour to kill at Stevenage, which I did with several large whiskies and two pints of disgusting ice cold beer. On the train to Leeds I carried on drinking with a boy who wanted to tell me what a great life it was in the Army. There's always one in every carriage. He could ski, sail, windsurf, scuba dive and kill with his bare hands – not bad for a lad of twenty two, eh? I fell asleep listening to his rib-tickling stories of how Shorty has planted one on the rupert who tried to tell him what was what in the heat and smother of the Gulf War. When we said goodbye, I noted we had drunk eleven cans and seven miniatures between us. Men with neat beards and little dictating tape recorders were looking at us askance.

"And I'm not surprise, you mad bugger," Gail's Dad said. He had been sent to the station to head me off. Tiny Tania had had a change of heart at the last moment and he had been deputed to sort something out. We got into his lopsided and freezing cold Lada and drove to his weekday local, where we gave the Timothy Taylor's an almighty pasting.

"You've a bloody rum idea of how to go on, Paddy, you have that."

"Patrick."

"Paddy'll do me. I bet you still haven't a ha'penny to scratch your arse with. But she has herself to think of."

"Do you still go to the Vollie?"

"You haven't hardly been gone a week," Frank scoffed. "Course we do. You have it to do, don't you?"

"Aye, lad, you do," I muttered drunkenly.

Which is more or less how I came to sleep on his lounge floor, wrapped in a sheepskin rug, with a devastated fish and chip supper congealing on the hearth beside me. During the night, men with bit and brace drills opened deep holes in my skull and filled them with quick-setting concrete. As a consequence, next morning I could hardly lift my head from the floor. Frank was studying form at Towcester, where there was a horse running called Gail's Secret. When I asked him the time, it was only half past seven.

"The wife won't come down until you've left. I did the wrong thing by bringing you home, seemingly. Bugger all else I could do, you were that puddled."

"Explain to her how I have been among strangers, Frank. I have supped with heathens. My heart was full last night."

"Aye well, sod off now, there's a good kid," he said.

I went into town and sent Diane, Tania and Frank a Christmas card each, bought a bottle of Famous Grouse at the supermarket and set off by train for Scarborough. I had need of the sea and the dusty solemnity of the Resident's Lounge at some elderly hotel; sleep, and a couple of good paperbacks to see me through the festive season. Of these, the sea was the most responsive to my need; I spent Christmas Day walking

148

along a turbulent South Bay, whipped by sand and spume, and experiencing every empty minute of it.

There are some things, I supposed in my innocence, that have a natural death to them. You meet, get involved, people tell you the most amazing or disgusting or exciting things; and then you part. You can't carry their load. They can't pick it up and carry it themselves. They are stalled.

I am stalled, I admitted to the mirror, before going down and meeting, as I had promised, the heart-broken widower from Pontefract who had tried to pick up the impossible burden of his wife's cancer death and had been brought to his knees by it. He was waiting for me in something called the Harbour Bar, and though I knew the exact timetable of this terrible thing that had happened to him, I realised that I had yet to ask him his name.

"A good walk?" he asked.

"Things to think about," I said gently.

On this table in front of him was a wallet of photographs of his wife. He stood, his knees trapped by the table's edge, an awful, beseeching half-smile on his face, afraid I would suddenly announce that I'd made a mistake and was invited out to dinner – that I wasn't like him, lonely and desolate, but bathed in love and companionship.

"I'll get some pints in, shall I? he said. "Take a peek at the snaps if you like – they're all of Jean, of course."

I picked up the wallet. Out in the main lobby of the hotel a man in a lavender blue jacket was playing Ivor Novello selections on the piano. Unaccountably, I found myself starting to cry.

TWELVE

When spring came around, I had a job at Gatwick, which was to watch, on behalf of some elderly and gullible Bristol solicitors, the comings and goings of a very bent junior partner of theirs. On their instruction, I followed him to Cyprus, where much of the client account he handled had found its way into bricks and mortar. He swam in the pool, while I sat in the grass overlooking his property, listening to the cicadas and admiring his girlfriend, a Canadian called Sky. Or was that Skye?

He went there most weekends. Such is the nature of mere work, as opposed to financial enterprise, I went there only once, to take a couple of rolls of film of the property and follow Sky about for half a day, just for the fun of it. The honest partners who had been left to slug it out in a chilly and rainy Bristol were outraged by the photographs I came back with. The pool and Sky's wanton toplessness in it were the last straw. But being solicitors they dealt with the situation cautiously. In the end the job span out to a whole month at an agreed per diem.

One Sunday night, waiting for him to fly in, I looked up

and saw Diane walking towards me. She was just off a flight from Tenerife, and looked thinner, browner, and more calm than I ever remember seeing her. Her hair was beautifully cut and she wore a pearl grey cardigan coat over trousers and a shirt. When I kissed her on the cheek, she smelt faintly salty, as though the Atlantic was just back there through those doors.

"How are you?"

"I'm okay," she said, "but you look like a cup of catsick. How's your lady in Yorkshire?"

"She's opening a Mexican restaurant with a very nice young man called Giles."

"There's a big call for that sort of thing up there, is there? Big expatriate Mexican community?"

"No, this is for the Yorkshire in-crowd, Diane. Of which we have our modest share. You know, trainee chartered accountants, trainee Next managers, building society clerks and the like."

"But your face didn't fit," Diane guessed.

"I never got the chance. I wasn't included on the menu."

"Oh dear. So who's looking after you?"

"I've been alone since I left you."

She nodded absentmindedly. I pressed her to a drink, which she refused. There was an uncomfortable few minutes while she lost her poise enough to linger when she should have swept away. She gossiped awkwardly about the Tenerife folk and a couple she'd met on the plane, every so often glancing at her watch. I felt an enormous pang of tenderness for her.

"How's old Goose Cottage?"

"Don't know. Haven't seen it for a fortnight."

"What happened? With Melissa? How did it work out?"

"Oh, you know," she said vaguely. "Okay. Everything's okay. But thanks for asking."

She kissed me briefly on the lips.

"I really must go," she said. But turned when she was twenty yards off and smiled.

"I found your other shoe, when the floods went away."

"Hang onto that, it's worth money," I called.

She was soon swallowed up by the tramping crowds. I warned to run after her, the way it happens in movies. But then, as you know, it never happens at Gatwick the way it does in the movies.

I had taken temporary accommodation in Crawley. It was a back bedroom that overlooked a forsaken allotment and was the kind of room that nobody supposes to exist anymore in this happy land, until human bones are discovered in the garden, or something of that sort. An electricity pylon hummed to itself in the middle distance, and on the horizon was a solitary tower block. There was an awful lot of muddy brown sky. My landlady was Mrs Lilley, a woman of such terminal melancholy that even the view from her back bedroom window could look jolly by comparison. Mr Lilley was the interesting one in the family. The year Celtic won the European Cup, he flew to Barcelona for the match and had yet to return.

"He wasn't even a Celtic supporter," Mrs Lilley told me when she got to know me better.

Most evenings I escaped the house to drink at the Half Moon, a huge roadhouse pub half a mile away. Between it and Mrs Lilley's house were two phone boxes. Admittedly they were both vandalised, but there was also one in the pub. They were encouragements to act on the chance meeting with Diane. I thought about it a lot, but did nothing.

The hot-shot young Bristol solicitor was finally arrested at his Clifton pied à terre, to the surprise of his neighbours, who considered him a very, very nice man. My final cheque was sent to Crawley with a scribbled note from the most senior partner saying that he would keep me in mind in future.

Meanwhile I was engaged on another modest enterprise, which was to drive a car and caravan to a permanent site in Ayr. The old fool who commissioned me to do him this small service knew what he was about: the car broke down twice even before I'd driven it as far as Preston. In Ayr, they had never heard of Mr Benson and his agreement to purchase a permanent pitch facing the race-course. I unhitched the caravan next to the toilet block and promised to be back, as soon as I had received further instructions from my client. I rang Diane on my way to a pint of heavy.

"I've driven all the way to Yorkshire to look for you," she said accusingly. The sweet tones of Gatwick were forgotten – she was back on track and I loved her for it.

"I told you, I don't live there anymore."

"Your card was the only way to track you."

"Christ, you didn't go to the address on it, did you?"

"They're your kind of people up there all right. You didn't tell me Tania was a circus dwarf. Where are you phoning from now?"

"Beldrummond Drive, Ayr."

"In Scotland?"

"Indeed."

"On holiday?"

"About to drive south."

"Well, make it soon. Make it now. I have to see you."

"Great!"

"You won't think so when you get here," she said.

"Don't hang up."

"Why?" she asked, after a pause.

I asked her to meet me in the Half Moon in Crawley the

153

following afternoon at two. I thought I was being reasonable, but she cut me off without so much as a goodbye.

We limped into Crawley at half past two, Mr Benson's Austin Maxi and me. I drove to the Half Moon, got out, and kicked the nearside front wing. Diane was watching me from her Tipo. It was a fine mild day and I absolutely insisted on buying her a drink. She followed me into the echoing saloon bar with wrinkled nose.

"How can you possibly live like this?" she asked.

"Like what? I don't live here, I just drink here. And anyway, did I say that I was an achieving sort of person? I'm a loser. I told you that. However, I do know many things about the Austin Maxi that might come in useful one day."

"You're a geek," Diane said.

There was no food to be had, of course. We carried our beer to a window table and looked out onto a row of broken saplings, behind which the traffic thundered.

"How much did this buffoon pay you to tow his caravan to Scotland?"

"He's a pensioner. Fifty, plus the petrol and expenses. How did you lose all that weight?"

"Tuna," she said succinctly.

We smiled and clinked glasses. But these were the hors d'oeuvres. The main dish was half to be expected. It took her no time at all to serve it up, piping hot. Melissa had gone missing again. I reached over and took her hand in mine.

"I'm telling you the honest truth when I say I've missed you and thought about you, Di. But all the rest of it has just evaporated, vanished. It wasn't my problem any longer and I've put it out of my head. Look at me, for Gods sake. I'm a man with international assignments on my hands. Scotland today, who knows where tomorrow?

"I need your help, Ganley."

"No you don't. The one thing I do remember about your damn daughter is that she can walk through muck and nettles ten feet high and come out the other side untouched. I even like her for it – that's on the occasions I'm feeling good about myself, too. But count me out."

"It's money," she suggested.

"Yes," I admitted. Diane watched me for a moment or two and then tried another tack.

"It isn't what she wants, it's what I want. I really did drive to Yorkshire for you and I'm here now."

"All right," I said. "Here's my opinion on your daughter as far as I can remember here. You have a kid who was badly done by. She should be at Oxford, breaking the heart of someone else's kid and experimenting with sex and ideas and clothes. Writing long essays in backward sloping handwriting and rubbishing films and novels. That's what she should be doing. But other things happened to Melissa and she's out there somewhere skating on thin ice. She may not be better off, but she's no worse off."

"Except for Westerman."

"Maybe."

"*Maybe?*"

I took her hand again and bounced it gently on the pub table.

"I don't know. Neither do you. She was raped. And her parents let her down."

"And now her life has been threatened."

I studied Diane. Her chin was up in that challenging way and her eyes were bright. She pulled her hand from mine.

"She rang me to say her life was being threatened, and two days later she disappeared."

"So you immediately rang the police."

155

"Oh come on, Patrick," she said, helpless.

We drove back to Goose Cottage with me at the wheel, Diane studiously looking out of the window. The little Tipo rocked as trucks vroomed past, hammering along the M25. Overhead, planeloads of Americans circled, silent and silvery against a faded denim sky. You sometimes look into other cars on the motorway and see mute couples, just driving, as though all talk had long ago been exhausted. That's how we drove back to Hertford.

She turned in the act of putting the key in the lock of the cottage door.

"I've missed you," she said simply.

Her lips were cold. After we had kissed and she went inside, I lingered by the door for a moment. The meadows I had last seen flooded were now a delicious green, and the river itself was what one imagines old England to have looked like when parsons went out with fowling pieces and milkmaids wandered along with stockings wetted with dew.

"I've missed *you*," I said.

Melissa had melted enough to come home to Mum for Boxing Day. They got blasted together and danced the merengue, recited De La Mare and Belloc, swapped diets, found they had always loved each other. Diane reminded her daughter there was a mound of money waiting for her as soon as business reopened after the Christmas break, and Melissa said yes, she was onto that one, and might take off travelling for a bit before going up to Oxford after all. Meanwhile, she wasn't quite ready to give up the job and London; and no, though she lived with a bloke – as Diane had already sneakily discovered – there was nothing heavy about it.

"Did you keep in touch?"

"Let me tell it my way," Diane chided. "She left here about three in the morning She was driving Zach's car. No license, no insurance or road fund tax, but I thought what the hell. She was happy."

"Did you talk to her about Westerman?"

She hesitated. The room was considerably tidier than as I remembered it. New pine bookshelves flanked the fireplace, and the piano lid was up. The carpets had been hoovered that morning.

"I couldn't bring myself to talk about it. You were right – the more questions you ask, the more you have to ask. I was just pleased to have her back. We arranged to phone once a week, and a couple of times I went up to take her out to lunch. All she ever talked about was Zach and a kitten they had, called Flaubert; restaurants, films, that sort of thing. It was wonderful."

"You'd got rid of me, you were losing weight, your New Year's resolutions were holding up…"

"Yes," Diane said simply. "She didn't talk about what Westerman did to her, or any of it. In the very worst of it, last Christmas, when Tony hired you, I thought I would lose her forever. But it seemed that I hadn't. It seemed, so long as I held my breath and prayed, I wouldn't."

"Did she also make her peace with Tony?"

"I imagine so."

Her lip was trembling. I pulled her to me and hugged her tight. Silly old murder could take a back seat when there was a kitten called Flaubert in the frame. When I released her, her eyes were wet with tears: I had understood that she could find life wonderful again without having to face the awkward corners in it. So here we were again, truants from the truth, stowaways on the dream express.

"I don't know what I want," she said to herself, helpless.

157

"You mean you're beginning to think its a mistake, having me back here."

She switched on a standard lamp and drew the curtains on the dusk outside.

"Zach rang me a fortnight ago. She had made an application for a passport. When it came through, she upped and left, taking all their money and the car. Without a word."

"That doesn't make her missing. She's just blown."

"Yes," Diane said, leaden. "Things have happened here too. I mean with Tony. He threw Pilar out."

I sat bolt upright.

"When was this?"

"March."

"You mean they quarrelled? He threw her out, showed her the door; or she left?"

"A girlfriend – an ex-neighbour – told me. There was a terrific scene, apparently. Half Hertford seems to know about it."

She was stroking the swell of her breast inside her shirt, a sure sign with Diane that a bombshell was on its way. Her eyes flicked across mine and then found something to examine on the Baluchi rug in front of the fire.

"Zach rang, like I said. The same day, Pilar rang to say Melissa should be very, very careful what she said or did."

"She rang here?"

"I was as amazed as you are."

"Wait a minute, Di. Melissa takes off, and the same day Pilar rings you up to what – warn you? Threaten you? How did Pilar know what the hell was happening?"

Diane glanced at her watch.

"Zach's coming to dinner tonight," she said. "I want you to talk to him."

"Oh, terrific," I wailed.

158

"He's a vegan," Diane added.

You would not have gone into the jungle with Zach. He was very tall and anorexic, with his hair tied back in a bun and little gold granny glasses on his putty nose. For a while he was going to be a poet – indeed, he left Stourbridge for Literary London as such as Johnson left Lichfield, with an actor for a friend. But Zach's friend was in no wise a Garrick. Only a month after arriving in the city of dreams, Zach's mate Andy took off for Berlin, where it was at these days, and to hell with theatre. Zach, meanwhile, soon found there was even less need of his poems in Hammersmith than his good-hearted old parents had warned. He stacked shelves in supermarkets and found the customers so gross that veganism was the only answer. Or the principal answer. Zach was also into being gay, but in the same miserably abstemious way. He was just one great gangling owl of a human being.

"I mean, everybody's, like, searching, but they don't know how to look. I sometimes just want to go up to people and say wake up, man. You know: wake up! Find yourself!"

"I hope you do," I said.

"It's impossible," he said sadly. "All the poison. The toxins inside everybody. There's poison everywhere. Lissa knew what I was talking about."

"I bet she did."

"How did you meet?" Diane asked.

"We found each other."

"Yes, but where, Zach?"

"In the street," he said. "I was having flute lessons from someone. Not all this James Galway stuff, but like real flute. Like traditional Indian flute. I was coming home and I saw Lissa. I experienced her aura in a really clear way. A really profound way. She was sitting on this wall, you know, just

159

absorbing things, the weather and everything. But with this really big aura."

"Fancy," Diane said gamely.

"And I didn't have a place to live just at that time, but she did, so we moved in together. She needed a house husband."

"She was already working in Wendell Street?"

"Yah," he said.

"Selling thrills on the phone Did you have an attitude towards that, Zacho?"

"Please don't call me Zacho," he said. "No, I didn't have an attitude towards it. It was something Lissa had to work out on her own. She had to relate to it in her own way."

"Didn't you and Mr Roskill make out together? Maybe he found a use for you in his organisation. Could I ring up and hear what happened when you met a big juicy plumber with a cock like a cucumber?"

He looked at me pityingly.

"You're being really pissy, man. You've never even met C.V. You don't know anything about him. You don't have any conception of what it is like to be me, either. You don't share any of the spaces I inhabit. Sure, the Wendell thing is bad, like a bad scene, I mean if you look at it one way. But Lissa rose above it."

"And anyway, one of you had to go out to work," I suggested.

He put down his spoon very carefully and turned to Diane.

"I don't have to take this," he said.

"Is it necessary?" Diane asked me.

"Okay. How about just answering some simple questions, Zach. Yes / no answers'll be fine. Have you ever met Roskill?"

"Yes, of course," he scoffed.

"He came to your place?"

"Yes."

160

"For dinner, that sort of thing?"

"Once or twice."

"And when that happened, did Melissa ever talk to him privately? Without you being present?"

"So?"

"Where?"

"In the bedroom."

"Where in the bedroom? On the bed?"

He whined incredulously.

"You're amazing, man."

"You mean you weren't listening at the keyhole?"

He shook his head wonderingly.

"Amazing."

"When was the last time you saw him?"

"The day before she left."

"You didn't connect the two things?"

"I mean, you're always looking at things in such a negative way. Lissa didn't like him all that much. But he was her boss. It was a job thing. If he came to check on the operation he had at the studios, he would call in after."

"So the last time he came, Lissa was upset?"

He shook his head.

"She gave you no inkling she was going? You woke up next morning and there she was, gone?"

"Exactly," he whined.

"Did you share the same bed, by the way?"

He glanced at Diane, who shrugged.

"We shared the same bed. So what? We were close friends. I mean were were really in tune with each other. What are you trying to find out?"

"I'm trying to find out what Mr Roskill said to her the night before she left, you dope. I'm trying to find out if Melissa said anything other than isn't the moon shiny, Zach? Or weren't those broad beans great?"

"Very funny."

"Roskill comes and has a little conflab with her, then he goes, then you get into bed together, and when you wake up, she's gone."

"That's it. That's what happened."

"I think it's extra-terrestials, Zach. I think she was abducted by little green men. For the life of me, I can't think of another explanation."

"Well, stuff you," he said, sulky.

But I had bottomed out with Zach. I put my face in his, my hands on his bony shoulders.

"The angel tattoo. What does that mean?"

He glanced nervously at Diane."

"It's okay, Zach," she said. "I know about it."

"It doesn't mean anything," he said doubtfully. "Mr Roskill did it. It's like a joke, his joke club."

"A sex club? Of adolescent girls?"

"A *joke*, man. He likes young people."

I turned to Diane and threw up my arms in exasperation. Her expression was curiously ambiguous. Although she wanted to find her daughter, she did not want to look for her here, along this line of questioning. She bit her lip.

"Liking young people isn't too difficult, Zach," she said, doubtful. "But tattooing Melissa was wrong."

Now it was his turn to throw up his hands. He wanted to indicate that he was young, we were old and wrinkled, that there are a great many things we might consider wrong that were just the way things happened. On my side, I wanted to shove his toothy snigger down into his pudding plate. That much got through to him.

"It's not a sex club. He talks about it as a joke. He calls it his Ladder of Angels."

"You mean he sells them?"

"Sells them?"

"Rents them, then. He's a pimp. He trades in them. Passes them round at parties, like cigarettes or chocolates. Come on, Zach. Wake up."

"Nothing like that," he said hotly. "He owns the chat-line business. What he does otherwise is his own look-out. Lots of men like younger people round them. You're really screwed up about this sex thing, aren't you?"

I gave way to impulse and wiped his face in his pudding. He did not resist. In a way he had been expecting it. And so had Diane. When his head came up, his gold-rimmed specs were coated with cream and crumbs of Black Forest gateau. Globs of it hung on his snub nose and whiskery little chin. He was massively dignified and passive about it all, and Diane was impressed. But I was so jumping mad, I threw my plate at the wall. Now she joined in the silent protest. The two of them sat there like people who have been told a politically incorrect joke, or witnessed rank bad form from a member of the lower classes.

"In Pontefract," I said shakily, "there was once a man called Denis, whose wife Jean was all his life. She went into hospital for a routine test and died of cancer of the liver and month later. Denis and Jean always went to Scarborough for the Christmas break – no kiddies, see?"

"What are you talking about?" Diane asked, taut.

"Shut up. On Boxing Day of last year, Melissa came up here with her tattoo and her job with spooky Mr Roskill and this gink for a bedtime companion. And though things were bad, they weren't that bad. You have to live in the world, after all. Not everybody who touches pitch is defiled by it."

"You are sick, man," Zach said.

"Don't speak, Zach. Don't dream of interrupting me. Not

163

if you want to keep your teeth. Up in Yorkshire on Boxing Day, Denis drove his VW to Flamborough Head. It's a beauty spot, with a coastguard station and big cliffs. Lots of birds – puffins, guillemots… Denis walked to the cliff-edge and talked to a nice family from Leeds. Birdwatchers. They thought him a very nice man. He waited until they went away with their binoculars and cagoules. And then he jumped."

I pushed back my chair and stood.

"Diane will tell you what a facetious bastard I can be. It isn't popular. I'm sorry to have assaulted you with a plateful of pudding. But if you don't start answering my questions I'm going to get really very unhappy. I'll start by breaking both your scrawny little arms."

"I've answered your questions," he yelped. "I can't help it if you're crazy. I haven't done anything wrong."

"Go upstairs and clean yourself up. Look at yourself in the mirror. You're young, Zach, and you're a very now person. But I could snap you in two like a pencil. Melissa's mother is worried that she is in real danger. You know – danger. Where hard characters come and put your eyes out, or cripple you for life. So when you come back downstairs, I want to hear exactly what Roskill said to her the night before she left. Got that?"

Far from threatening her, Roskill had come to warn her. Zach had listened at the door of the bedroom and heard him plead with her to go, before it was too late. He had actually cried. But Zach, weak little nothing that he was, had not been able to tell Melissa what he had overheard. He got into bed beside her and lay fearful and weepy, willing her to tell him what was going on. She stroked him absently, her eyes wide open, her breathing calm and regular. In the morning she was gone.

"Who have you had round to the house since?"

"What?" he asked, weeping now.

"Who has come to look for her? Was it an Indonesian woman called Pilar?"

"Who?" he asked, bewildered.

"Was it a nasty man called Denzil, who wanted to shove your head up your arse, unless you told him where she was?"

"Oh God," Zach moaned.

Denzil had taken the kitten Flaubert and put it into the oven on gas mark 5. At last I felt sorry for the poor kid. I poured him a brandy and held his head up. Diane was backed up against the wall, her eyes filled with terror.

"I don't know what she's done," Zach sobbed, throwing his arms round me, the snot from his nose wetting the front of my shirt.

"It's okay," I said. "You got it out. You were frightened, but you got it all out. It's all over now. They won't hurt you. Come on, Zach. Be a man."

I looked across at Diane and my heart melted. When she cried like this, her face began to come apart as a readable identity. Crying, her personality dissolved and all that was left was the quick, the raggedy heart. I have seen that happen a hundred times, in places a hundred times more awful than Diane's sitting room with the ruined meal and the sobbing boy hanging round my neck. But the effect is always the same. When you see it, you cannot tolerate the pain. The one thing you cannot do, is turn your back. If you could, the world would have rolled to a stop many centuries ago.

I made coffee, went upstairs and showered, cleaned my teeth, turned my socks inside out and brushed my sweater with her hairbrush. Rolled deodorant, splashed cologne, dressed, went downstairs and held out my hand. Zach was asleep, his head among the dishes. She pulled herself out of the chair without daring or wishing to take my eyeline. I walked

165

to the kitchen door and opened it. A crisp, fresh gust of wind entered, smelling of the garden and the dewy fields beyond. Waited while she hunted and fiddled, held out my hand again, and she put the keys to the Tipo into my palm. She watched me go without a word.

THIRTEEN

The Peppercorn Café had folded. That upset me as much as anything else that had already happened in this whole sorry story. Lawrence and Julia and baby Penn were somewhere else, queuing up with the rest in some benefits office, waiting to talk to a clerk behind his protective glass. The little café was wiped out, its windows pasted with fly sheets advertising pub rock and political rallies. Just inside the door was a tiny mountain of uncollected mail. Someone – maybe Lawrence – had smashed the serving counter down and spread it around the floor. All the electrics were back to the bare wires. Nobody was in any hurry to rush in to fill the gap left by those two and their puny little baby with his Peruvian wool bonnet.

Across the road, Roger's house was likewise untenanted. The ground floor windows and the front door were secured by half-inch chipboard and there was barbed wire wound round the down pipes. It didn't hit me the same way. I sat in the Tipo for a while and smoked a cigarette, before reversing round the corner into Toft Place and heading back north. The M1 was some kind of anaesthesia, and I drove for hour after hour,

167

stopping only for petrol and cigarettes. I didn't ring Diane until I was brought awake by the glorious country of the Upper Teesdale Valley.

"Where are you?" she asked.

I looked out of the phone box at bare hills basking in sunlight.

"This has got personal, Di," I said.

"What happened? What did she say?"

"I'm on my way to Roskill first."

"Let me come with you."

"No," I said slowly, watching the cloud shadows chasing each other across honey landscape and wondering if this was how people actually did go mad. "It's personal. I'll be back in a couple of days."

"A couple of days?"

At Larne, Diane's car was separated from the other ferry traffic and waved to an open ended shed. As I pulled in, a burly policeman made bulkier by a flak jacket ambled over. The muzzle of his machine gun rested on the edge of the window. His sidekick covered me across the bonnet of the car.

"Have ye onny identification on youse, bucko? Is it in the glove compartment is it? Then take it out real slow, will ye? Is it a wee holiday, or what?"

"Just the Antrim coast."

"And where will ye be staying?"

"I'm a tourist. I'll be touring."

He studied me with a falsely genial expression, under his black cap his drinker's face concealing a shrewd instant assessment. But he was a serious drinker all right. His lips were pale, almost lavender blue. He flicked the driver's license with his free hand and read the name with a smile.

"Mr Patrick Ganley, is it? Me uncle Jack was a Ganley. But

that was in Clitheroe. In Lancashire. No relation, I don't suppose."

"Been through it once. Didn't stop."

"Are you a golfer or something like that, Mr Ganley?"

"I'm here for the crack," I said.

"You'll find plenty of that, so you will."

I drove up the Antrim coast, along the exquisite shoreline road, passing only one other car, and with an sensation of having entered a time-warp. Perhaps England had been like this once, in point of calm: it was difficult to imagine this largely empty landscape where I had seen more cormorants than people bearing all the terrors of a civil war. At a bar called MacBrides in a little village of council houses and fat cat villas, I drank a couple of Guinnesses, chased by a couple of Bushmills.

I meandered the last miles to Ballycastle through wonderful low sunlight, streaming across the dark green fields and turning the sea molten silver. My eyes were itching and the road ahead buckled gently – motion sickness from the driving and the ferry crossing. I thought of pulling over to sleep for an hour. But as they say over here, that wouldn't be it at all. I had somewhere I had to go.

The house was nothing very much at all and may have been the Ulsterman's childhood home. It was a white stucco manse up a gravel drive, with laurels sprawling over the spiky lawns. Where once there had been a view of the bay and the eighteenth century fairway of the golf club, there was now, blocking the way, a long, low tyre and exhaust depot. The borders to the garden were empty, but a couple of wan lights burned inside the house and there was a Peugeot in the drive. I rang for admittance on a Victorian bell-pull hanging half off the wall.

Peter Pelling's friend Roger opened the door to me, dressed

in his kimono, and zonked out of his brains on something prescribed by a good doctor. His expression was utterly blank: he didn't recognise me and had trouble with my voice even, as though I were speaking in Urdu or Icelandic. It was not until a familiar face appeared at his shoulder that I was admitted. Roskill shepherded the old man away down the hall with gentle patting motions and indicated over his shoulder that I should go into what turned out to be a study. The room smelt of damp leather and cigar smoke.

"He's on the pills, you've noticed. The tranquillisers, so they call them. But I don't suppose you've come to talk to him, have you? That wouldn't be your noble Christian purpose at all."

To begin with, he spoke so softly I could hardly understand what he was saying. Nor did it help that he liked to lecture. He spoke in unhurried sentences with the vanity of someone who lives mostly alone and is seldom contradicted A surreal touch was provided by his clothes. He wore two unbuttoned cardigans and on his head he sported a fake astrakhan fur hat.

"You'd be Mr Ganley, of course, from the fearless side of the water. Who's taken the trouble to come to the Province to see how we are over here. Nice of you to call in without a bit of a word to say you're coming. But then that wouldn't be your style either."

"Is Roger all right?"

"Is he all right? He's a sad and desperate man. The death of his friend, you understand. I brought him across, sure, for medical reasons and a chance to recoup. Did he put your nose out of joint just now, did he? I'm sure he recognised you but would rather not waste his breath on you. It was me you really wanted to see, Mr Ganley, I don't doubt that for a moment. You have the light of battle in your eyes, as we might say. I

170

won't offer you a drink because you won't be staying that long."

"Was this your mother's house, Mr Roskill?"

His eyes flashed angrily for a second – sparked briefly with hatred – and then died. He picked up his cigar from an ashtray and examined the tip. It was still lit.

"You're a foolish sort of man, so you are. I've heard that said of you by others. Yes, this was my mothers' house. My father was a pig of a man who was offed by the boys. A bit of a problem he had with them back in the war. That was in Belfast, when he was a contractor for the yards. So your instinct's a good one. I'm a mums boy, so I am. Now what do you make of that?"

He held out his bony and none too clean hands to a little coal fire, seemingly at his ease with me and all mankind. His smile indicated that he was sailing close to the wind and enjoying it. The little spat of anger had been a mistake, the smile seemed to be saying. I was a lightweight and he need hardly trouble himself to conceal what he thought of me. His mother's photograph portrait loomed down from the wall. It was of a large woman with piercing black eyes. She wore some sort of chain of office around her neck.

"Has Roger been here ever since he attempted suicide?"

"What would you care?"

"And you've looked after him all this while?"

"I'm a bit of a saint to my friends," he said.

"What does he know?"

Roskill looked genuinely confused.

"What does he know about what?"

"The Ladder of Angels, for example."

"Oh dearie me," he chuckled. "Now what have we uncovered here, I wonder?"

"I'm looking for Melissa."

171

"And you think she's upstairs with a cork and a couple of feathers in it stuck up her arse, chained to the bed? Not so, Mr Ganley. You are free to go and look if you will."

"Tell me about your Angels."

"Oh, I would, wouldn't I? I'd be sure of some understanding from the likes of you. You're an unpleasant bit of stuff, Mr Ganley. And I would say a lazy man, a lazy sod of a fellow. I don't have Angels. I'm not the pimp you take me for, it's not that sort of business at all."

"But there are Angels."

"You've got me foxed, bucko."

"I have a client, Diane and Tony Pelling's daughter. Melissa. One of your employees in the sex-chat business. Gone missing after threats from you."

"I know Melissa," he said. "What threats were these?"

"She has a tattoo of yours. Of an angel."

"On her titties. Correct. She showed it you, did she?"

"Don't get up my nose too quickly, Roskill. I talked to the gink she lived with in Shepherd's bush, to Zach. He told me about the Ladder of Angels idea. Maybe that's just part of life's rich pattern to you, but wrapped up in this are two murders."

"Whose was the other one?" Roskill asked mockingly.

"And an inheritance of half a million pounds."

He pursed his lips in an even greater display of indulgent good humour.

"You're not a rich man yourself, are you, Mr Ganley? And if you'll forgive me for saying so, not an achieving sort of a fellow either. So I'll just point out to you that the money's a bit of a side issue here. The money's not a lot. These two murders you talk of now. Our friend Peter Pelling was killed by the boys that don't like his sort. That's my theory. He was an old queer that made a mistake too many on a dark night. The police – let's put a good construction on it, shall we? – the police are alive to all the possibilities."

"But without having made an arrest as yet."

"Aye," Roskill said, grave. "The overworked and under-paid Met. D'you think it's because they're baffled for a motive, do you? We'll see. It seems as plain as day to me. But anyway, I plead innocent. Was the other one Dr Westerman?"

It came to me: talking to Roskill was much like talking to a vain and elderly priest.

"Do you know who killed him?"

"If I did, it would be my public duty to make those suspicions known, wouldn't it now? But unfortunately for you, the man was killed down there in France, a place I've never been. I'm a home bird, Mr Ganley. Anyone round here would tell you that."

"Let's cut all this crap. Who tattooed Melissa?"

Roskill laughed.

"A very nice man in Coleraine. With a business of that sort, down there by the bridge. D'you mean who paid for it? I did. There's no Gothic horror for you to discover here, bucko. There's no castle dungeons and boxes of Transylvanian earth. It's a tattoo, done by a tattooist, who has a bit of a license for carrying out the work from the health people. I can fix you up with the same, next time you're in Antrim."

"Melissa agreed?"

"Considering where it's placed, she'd have to agree, don't you think? Grow up, man. She was on for it, of course she was."

"You don't seem to think it was important."

"Me? I've no tattoos. You must ask her. She'll maybe tell you she thought it was adult."

"When in fact it was puerile."

"Puerile," Roskill mused. "What a way with words you

173

have, Mr Ganley. Do you think I talked her into it? I paid for it, was all. Your man Uncle Peter egged her on to do it."

I stared at him in amazement. Roskill sniggered.

"The nice cultured old toff from Trinity College Cambridge. That's the man we're talking about. His idea of a wicked wheeze. Can you believe it? I'm just an old Prod from a grammar school. It's not my style at all. Did you think there were dozens of wee girls walking about with tattoos on their tits, all owned and operated by me? I bet you did. You've a vivid imagination."

The door opened and Roger looked in on us, as if trying to remember where he was, and what the hell he was doing there. Roskill jabbed his thumb at the zombie.

"Ask Roger. Melissa's Uncle Peter was a fool. He was a terrible old reprobate. Wasn't that it, Roger? Wasn't your man Peter just the fellow to make a three act opera out of a cheap thrill? A silly old fart of a man who liked to play at being vicious and perverted? The master of ceremonies for anyone he could rope in?"

"Peter," Roger managed to dredge up.

"That's who we're talking about. I'm telling Mr Ganley here, how I'm a business man and nothing else."

"What about Peter?" his former lover asked, frowning. Roskill turned to me.

"Don't mind him, he's this way always. The address was handy and that's how I came to meet them, the pair of them. Your man Peter saw himself as a bit of a poet of evil. God knows he talked enough and loved himself enough to fit the bill."

"But you do like young girls, Roskill."

Roskill nodded negligently.

"I'm saying, it was handy. The address was given to me by friends of theirs. You're coming on like an idiot again, Mr

Ganley. I like the green fruit, yes, but you're enough a man of the world—"

Roger turned and left the room, his kimono rustling. He shut the door behind him with exaggerated care. Roskill shook his head.

"The poor man is in a hell of a state."

"You were saying, about me being a man of the world."

"Yes. You knew already, long before you ever met me face to face, that some people have certain needs that the majority don't share. You don't like people like me – but then you knew that, too, a long time ago. Unfortunately, we can't just go away, now, can we?"

"You're saying that Peter Pelling introduced you to Melissa?"

"See now, there you go again. Introduced me – what does that mean? I met her there in London, yes. I had no interest in her, not in a sexual way: none at all. But she's an original all right. A dreamer like her uncle, in a way. Twice as vain, begod. But not my type. I could see she was clever – and she is one hell of a clever-cuts, no doubt of that. But hardly a child would you say? Hardly a little innocent. Peter, it was, who teased and tormented the life out of her, until out of bravado she's away to Coleraine to the tattoo shop."

"I don't believe you, Roskill."

"Whether you do or whether you don't is all the same to me."

"Did Roger take part in all this?"

"Not a great man for the pleasure. Roger went along with it. In their heyday they were somebody, the two of them. Their *salon*, I mean. You know, magistrates, headmasters, vicars. Little boys and girls, lots of fun and games. Oh, back in the fifties when they were young, they were a pair of devils. Roger was the quiet one, who looked after the money."

175

He walked to a bureau and unlocked it, withdrawing identical green exercise books.

"Their diaries. God knows what else there might be in that house, the rubbish they hoarded. I burned a lot of the stuff. I'm giving you a sight of these to get you off my back, Mr Ganley."

I flicked through a few pages of the topmost one. It was largely addresses and nicknames, bits of doggerel and crude drawings of children. It was all impossibly seedy.

Roskill was watching me without the slightest discomfort. And why not? This was the sort of book kept by smutty schoolboys.

"Were they still active when you met them?"

"They were pathetic old fools. But there are certain ways of life where you can't exactly choose the quality of your friends. They were known around the town, as Pelling would have it."

He laughed.

"They were well enough known for their address to be a secret," he added.

"Did Melissa know what they were up to?"

"I don't think so," Roskill said. "I wouldn't say Melissa was exactly well versed in the ways of the world, would you?"

"She's no fool."

"That much is true. I gave her a job because she's as bright as a button. Not your kind of work again, is it, Mr Ganley? But a job. It was a mistake, in that it fetched you here to queer things. But if you're worried about her, I wouldn't be. She's a sublime innocent, is that one."

"So that in all this with her uncle, you were just an amused bystander," I suggested.

"Amused is the word."

"And what about the threats?"

But before he could answer, the door opened again and

Roger came back in. In his right hand, hanging down like a provincial rep prop, was an old service issue .45. The lanyard was still attached and trailed to the ground, the loop making a trap for his chequered slippers. Roskill glanced.

"You see the effect you're having, Mr Ganley, on ordinary people. You're muddying the waters, making things messy."

"Peter," Roger said. It came out as a demand.

"Yes, yes, Peter. Peter isn't here, don't you see, you poor man? This is another fellow altogether."

"Shouldn't you get the gun away from him?"

"It's a game we play," he muttered uneasily. "Melissa wasn't one of my conquests. The man we've been talking about thought it was a great gas to pretend she was. They were two of a kind. Each could talk the hind legs off a donkey. The games people play, Mr Ganley. The whole bloody family was nothing but a great pain in the arse, so it was. As to whether you believe me or not, I don't have to assure you of anything, or convince you of anything. In fact, shit on you, you wee man."

Roger seemed to be following a different script. He took one more step into the room and raised the ancient pistol with a wavering hand.

"Don't harm him now," Roskill called.

Roger brought his other hand up to steady his aim. The skies outside had grown dark and he loomed in the doorway, his outline blurred by the bags and folds of his kimono. For some reason, God knew why, Roskill took off his hat.

"Don't be an arse now, Roger, there's a good man."

Roger blew off one side of the Ulsterman's smile, and with it the lower jaw. The bullet was diverted in its trajectory and smacked into the wall a foot from my own hand. The sudden blush of warmth I felt on my face and neck was Roskill's blood. He lay on the floor, his eyes trying to focus, a fountain nearly a foot high spurting from his collar.

177

Roger looked at me with an expression of calm complicity. He cocked his head very slightly, as if listening. He smiled lopsidedly and put his finger to his lips. There was something we shared in the is horrible moment. Then it came to me what the secret something was: though we were deafened by the report, we could both hear Roskill's shoes drumming on the dusty carpet.

"Go now," Roger said.

He pointed the revolver negligently in my direction. I stepped over Roskill and edged past his killer. Upstairs there was a bathroom with a brown bath and basin. I found a sliver of soap and washed the blood from me with shaking hands and then cleaned myself on a threadbare bath towel. I looked out of the window and saw that the back garden abutted the churchyard. Beyond that was a sort of square, with cars parked in it, one of them Diane's. It was almost dark. Young boys in moth white T-shirts were playing football with a crumpled lager can.

On the back of the bathroom door was a heavy wool sweater. I pulled it over my head. Downstairs, Roger had begun amusing himself by shooting out the glass in the windows. He was right. It was time to go. I could see the police coming down the hill in two reinforced and armoured Land Rovers. They were not stinting on the accelerator pedal.

FOURTEEN

I sailed back to Stranraer two days later with a Glasgow boys' boxing team that had been less than victorious in a tour of the Six Counties. String bean kids sulked at the fruit machines or gazed open-mouthed and expressionless at the sea. Their officials, tubby men in pink blazers and pearl slacks, wasded about with trays of pints, cursing the day they'd ever founded the club, let alone organise the bloody tour. The President wore a gimcrack chain of office and was a huge ox of a man with an old pro's frown on his face. He sat at a littered table, seeming to listen to the conversations round about, but splitting matches with his thumbnail and going walkies with his mind. He was pointed out to me by a worried tub of lard called Jackie McEvoy.

"Right enough, Big Des's heartbroken. D'you see him sitting there? The man is gutted, no mistake about that. I always say tae the lads – if y'box for Winston Cross ABC, y'box for the big yin."

"And he's been around this game, eh?"

"Been around?" Jackie scoffed. "The man's a household word, pal. Yay've seen him on television. More than once."

179

But the boys from Winston Cross were not the main attraction on the ferry. A couple of dozen strangely silent young men formed a huge group in one corner of the bar, their baby faces sullen. Though they wore T-shirts and jeans, preposterously oversized bomber jackets and all the rest of the tat, they were squaddies, and everyone knew they were squaddies. The curse of the Six Counties lay on them too. They drank little and stared at the boxers with real loathing. Here was the life they'd left behind. They were hoping against hope a wrong word might be said, a drink spilled. In fact, like religious zealots, they were willing destruction and the end of the world, to commence here and now, with no quarter given. And, like miserable sinners, the boy boxers were drawn to the same idea, but from the opposite end of the argument. They were ready to give themselves up to apocalypse. They plotted in the sick-drenched lavatories as to how to achieve it. We were in a lower level of hell here.

But the bar staff had been around a bit, too. They closed the bar half an hour early.

"Why weren't you arrested?" Tony Pelling wanted to know.

"I didn't shoot him, remember? And I don't think the police needed much help with their enquiries. But that's three murders, Mr Pelling. That's quite a lot for one family."

I had asked him to meet me in Carlisle. We sat on the bed in his motel room, listening to the traffic going south down the M6. The people in the next suite were elderly Canadians from the Peace River country. They were playing their treasure trove of taped bagpipe music and either dancing of threshing about like stags in rut. It was making Pelling jumpy. He licked his tortoise lips.

"And all this stuff about Peter? Do you think that can really be true?"

I gave him my most level stare.

"What's this, National Artless Comment Day? I think we both know how true it can be. It's just that you forgot to tell me. Was that where you went, really, when you said you were going to your dinner club in Cambridge?"

"Christ, you just never stop, do you? The dinner club is real. The people in it are real. This other thing – I had nothing to do with it. I hated Peter's guts. I did everything possible to hide what he was from my family."

"Not all that successfully. Your brother's dead, your pal Westerman's dead and now the very wonderful C.V. Roskill is dead. And flitting around all these corpses like the fairy on the Christmas tree is your dopey daughter. Some story, for a chartered and incorporated wimp from the leafy lanes of Hertford."

"Did you get me up here to insult me?"

"I got you up here to see whether you'd come."

"I was on my way anyway, to help Roger."

"Bullshit."

He wobbled his adam's apple and looked out of the grimy window. Next door, the Canadians were singing 'The Flower of Scotland' – or one was. The woman was singing 'Will Ye Stop Your Tickling, Jock'. While we watched, an empty bottle of the Macallan flew from their window and landed noiselessly in the scratty grass of the motel compound. The Scottish Tourist Board could be proud of them.

"I came to find out what you want," Pelling muttered.

"Right. Now I'm going to spell a few simple things out for you. The police found Roger with a smoking gun in his hand and Roskill dead on the floor. That's open and shut murder. Once he's been emptied of all the shit inside him they'll find him fit to plead. There'll be a trial, Mr Pelling – learned counsel, the panoply of the law, all that. Or, putting it another way, public crucifixion. Yours, not his. The Press will nail you and

181

yours up. You won't know what hit you."

"What can *I* do about it?" he whimpered, wringing his hands.

"Let's start by telling the truth. In the days of his gilded youth, your half brother ponced around London running some kind of sex ring. Yes or no?"

"Yes," Tony Pelling said after a long pause. "He – I suppose he thought of himself as some kind of libertarian. He knew a lot of people of like mind. There were parties, and so on. It was very pathetic, all of it. You say a sex ring: that makes it sound terrible. He was a fantasist, a dreamer. He was a bloody fool, in other words."

"Did you go to any of these parties?"

"Of course not."

"Did you take advantage of any of his contacts?"

"No."

"Never?"

"No," his said, more slowly.

"You better tell me."

"No. The answer is no," he said, anguished. "The sky is going to come tumbling down, isn't it?"

"We can be pretty certain of that. Did your wife or Melissa know all this about Peter?"

"I don't think so. Diane knew he was a shit, of course. Melissa was innocent of it all."

"Until recently."

"I thought it had all burnt itself out," Pelling sobbed, his head in his hands. "I thought it was all in the past. He had some sort of a scare, in the seventies. There was a cover up of some kind. It's no use asking me the details, because I never knew them. But he overstepped the mark in some way and he was lucky to stay out of the courts. As a consequence, it quietened down."

"You say you met Westerman in Tangier."

"I did. By chance. I told you. By *chance*."

"But there is a photograph of him with Roger and Roskill taken on the Backs. Which you took."

"That was *after* I met him. I told you how that happened."

"You and Bob were on your way to tea with some blameless academic for a chat about the meaning of meaning when you trip over your brother's boyfriend and a strange Ulsterman stretched out on the grass?"

"Yes."

"Try again."

"You've seen the photograph," Pelling said, uneasy.

"I have. It's a lovely little study. I love it. But let me give you another scenario—"

Pelling jumped to his feet and left the room. I thought he was going to run – bolt, scurry away and jump into his car. He had the stiff legged urgency of a man in flight. But he was merely going along the motel corridor to bang furiously with his bony fists upon the door of the carousing Peace River people in the next room.

"Will you kindly stop this infernal racket?" he bellowed.

The door opened and a burly naked man in his seventies, with more blue than pink in his skin colour, stepped out and without introductions of any kind clouted Pelling around the ear. The accountant fell to the ground like a sack of coals.

"Up yours, buddy," the man from Peace River said. He stared at me, plucked at his ancient and raggy groin and silently invited me to get bashed, too. He was yanked back into the room by his wife's plump and freckled arm and the door slammed. Pelling sat up, his knees round his chin, scrabbling for his glasses on the tastefully neutral nylon carpet...

"He hit me," he said, nearly in tears. "You saw it, he struck me."

"Come back in here and stop provoking people, you gink," I said. "Open your damn fridge and get me a drink. And do yourself a favour. Start telling the truth."

They *had* gone to Tangiers, and they *had* shared a girl who worked for the BBC and who might or might not be a researcher. But that was after their first meeting. That had happened in the following very predictable way: Pelling was mooning about in Cambridge, dreaming of firm flesh and wishing he'd read even half the books his friends in the dining club mentioned over their bouef en daube, when he chanced upon Westerman, Roskill and Roger having a day out. One thing lied to another and they all pitched up at a farmhouse out beyond the Gog Magog hills, drinking kir and misbehaving badly with some little friends of the farmer-squire, who was called Toby Waldorf.

"That's why the other three were there, of course. This bloody man Waldorf was nuts. He was certifiable. There must have been forty people there. It was ostensibly a barbecue. I didn't even notice what was happening to begin with. Boys appearing from nowhere, I mean."

"Just boys?"

"Some girls," Pelling muttered, sullen. "And women."

"You all chipped in a few quid," I suggested.

"Yes," he said, staring at me with loathing. "There was a charge. You're so bloody clever, aren't you? It started as a barbecue, I'm telling you. There was a pool. We'd all had a great deal to drink. When it really got going I was confused. I don't care whether you believe me or not. But Westerman seemed different. We talked a lot. We sat in the kitchen while all this was going on and we talked."

"About a single European currency, that sort of thing?"

"I just can't tell you how much I despise you, Ganley.

184

What pleasure do you get from torturing people like this?"

"Listen, you pathetic streak of piss. Someone *killed* Westerman. You sat talking to him in a kitchen, which you want me to see as a little haven of goodness in a naughty world. Good old Westerman, for hanging onto his trousers and his self-respect, while all around others are losing theirs. A man to admire. Then he rapes Melissa. Then he's dead."

Pelling lay with his head on the table they always provide in motels. There was a knock at the door. When I opened it, the Peace River man was standing there in a tartan dressing gown.

"I came back to say sorry. My wife says to say sorry. We'd like to invite you for a drink."

"Well, we're in the middle of a business meeting."

He patted my face with a drunk's tenderness.

"I know. We've been listening through the wall with a tooth glass."

He laughed uproariously, saluted Pelling, and staggered off back down the corridor. Finding the fire extinguisher an impediment to his progress, he took it off the wall and carried it in to show his wife.

"The whole world is mad," Pelling said.

"Let's just concentrate on your part in it. Westerman picked you up at this party. Or you fell in love with the big lunk. One way or another, you opened the door that led sooner or later to your daughter. To whom something dreadful happened. Then Westerman just happens to be killed while you and she just happen to be in the area."

"That's it. That's all it is."

"Okay."

"Well, what do you want me to tell you?" Pelling screamed.

"Tell me why Pilar left."

"Pilar? *Pilar?*"

He scrubbed furiously at his temples as though the

185

madness he detected in the world was attacking him through the bones of his skull. I knocked his hands away.

"Last Christmas time, I asked you why you arranged to meet Westerman in France. You told me some cock and bull story about being friends, about giving Melissa a break at the same time. Just a cosy threesome."

"Well?"

"I don't think so. You knew nothing about what had happened between Westerman and your daughter. I believe you. But Westerman did. I don't see him as rushing down to Angoulême to meet his victim. So, he had to have another reason for coming. I can think of one straight off the bat. He thought he'd find you on your own."

Pelling's eyes were shifting about.

"This is beside the point."

"Is it hell. Together you could go out and have boys' fun. Your money and his French. To look on your own contribution in what I guess was its usual light. That was the idea, wasn't it? But then someone – and I'm guessing it was Pilar – talked you into taking Melissa. At the very last moment, maybe. I would like to have been there to see that."

He sat on the bed. Then he rolled onto his side and drew his knees up to his chest in the classic foetal position. I lit a cigarette and switched on afternoon television. Ruby Keeler peered out at me in satin shorts and a sailor vest.

"Turn that off," Pelling moaned. "Please."

"I don't care in the least mind that Roskill is with us no longer. But Westerman's different. You're too stupid to be guilty of anything like murder, Mr Pelling. You're just a weak little man who keeps his brains in his underpants. But even you don't think Westerman was mugged for his money by petty crooks on the ramparts. Deep down in your heart of hearts, which is a dusty little cubbyhole indeed, you think one of two

186

people killed him: Melissa, or Pilar. You don't know how, exactly, but that's what keeps you awake at night. Isn't it?"

"I don't want to talk about it."

"You get on with your regressing. I'll watch the movie. We're not leaving here until you do want to talk about it."

Now there were twenty hoofers in satin shorts and backless chiffon blouses, every one of them convinced she was able to dance better than Ruby, mugging the camera as they taptapped their plump little bodies past the director. I thought of them as they were today, crazy old ladies with poodles and a few publicity stills – and the precious video of themselves at twenty, shining out of the black and white world that was forever 1935, their breast jumping, their legs kicking.

It was growing dark when he sat up and asked for a drink of water. He had slept for a while and was now quite rational. In a calm, matter-of-fact voice, he told me what I wanted to know. It was quite simple, once he had brought himself to utter it. He had met Pilar in a London hotel, where she was a receptionist. He had never seen anyone more beautiful or desirable. She was the stuff of his dreams.

I knew all this. It was a matter of waiting for him to say the rest: he held the glass of water against his temple to calm the throbbing vein there. The meeting had not been by chance. Westerman had introduced them.

"You mean Westerman had been there before you. You poor sap."

"Your contempt is well-merited," Pelling said, sitting in the dark with the headlights flaring in the grimy window behind his head. "I'm the weakling you describe me as. For him she was just a whore – an expensive and troublesome one, but a tart all the same. I was supposed to see her the same way."

"He was just passing her on. He was marking your card for a good thing."

"Maybe. Yes. I had the money to buy her for a night or two and then forget her. I could even have developed a sort of client relationship with her, someone to see and turn to when in London. Instead, I fell in love with her. That should amuse you, Ganley. You're a student of human weakness. I wanted her forever."

He took his glasses off and polished them on his tie, wincing. The headlights swept past relentlessly, backlighting his narrow skull, his long neck. I thought of him the day he tried to tell Pilar she was the only girl in the world for him. I tried to imagine where this had happened, the look on her face as he stumbled out his declaration of love.

"What did Westerman make of that?"

"He was amused. They were all amused."

"Who are they?"

He shrugged.

"She knew Roskill. She had a set of her own – clubbers, some Arabs, girls like her. I never asked too many questions. You can have no idea: not because you're any better than me, any more sane or balanced. You're crazy, too. Anybody can see that about you. But you're poor. Diane was right about you – you come cheap. I had the money and the willingness to buy her for good. They were laughing at me, but Pilar instinctively knew that much about me. She knew she could get away, get clear. And that's what she wanted."

I thought of the conversations I'd had in the pub with her the previous Christmas and nodded. Pelling smiled sadly.

"I thought it was a way of ending all the foolishness in my life That was a bonus of the situation, of course, an afterthought. Because rational considerations hardly came into it. I was utterly besotted with her. She was a weakling's dream

188

come true. I could enslave myself to just one woman. Which is what I tried to do."

He switched on the light and we sat staring at each other. He walked to the drinks cabinet and took out two miniatures of whisky.

"She is not a stupid woman. She always acts very cautiously, with a great deal of circumspection. She listened to me and understood me for what I was. There was Melissa to consider. On the other hand, I simply had to have her. She came to me as housekeeper after Diane left, and when Melissa went to University, the plan was that we would marry. I do believe that is what she wanted for herself. And so it would have been. Except for Westerman."

"She found out what he had done to Melissa?"

"Yes," Pelling said.

"She summoned Roskill."

"I suppose so. Yes."

"She was frightened that you would see the light and dump her. That she would be tarred with the brush of having known all this riff-raff, of getting you into all this mess and that you'd get rid of her. She'd lose what she'd got."

"Yes."

I phoned for a sandwich. Pelling took his drink back to bed and lay face down, his hands over his head.

"You wanted to know why I kicked her out," he said, his voice muffled.

"I know why you kicked her out. Because you finally worked out that she'd had Westerman killed for you, and you couldn't live with it."

It was an idea, the cast of a fly over a dark pool.

Pelling did not move. He did not speak. I stood over the bed watching him, thinking of Pilar, her neat, lithe body, the sense she gave out of ruthless self-seeking. Pelling's shoulders

189

heaved as he wept silently into the pillow.

"Is that what happened? Pelling?"

When he did not answer, I picked up the keys to the car and threw three green exercise books down on the bed beside him.

"Roskill gave me these. You better destroy them. There's nothing there to incriminate you or yours, except for your own name, a long time ago."

Still he didn't move. I shrugged.

"She came to you out of choice, Pelling. And you are right, she never did anything without thinking about it first. It means she wanted you."

"Go to hell," he whispered.

On the way out, I passed the kid who was taking the sandwich to Room 37. She was about Melissa's age, but blithe and artless. She was singing as she went. I pushed open the door at the end of the corridor and stepped out into the windy and noisy night. I needed cigarettes, but could not bear to go back in and feel the pain of the place engulf me yet again.

FIFTEEN

I wanted to search his house alone, using the key Diane still had. But she insisted on coming with me. We lit many lamps, switched on the radio and television and generally made ourselves at home. We could be overlooked by at least two of the neighbours, and the sandy lanes outside were a popular route for dog walkers. It was better to bluff it out. But I did not like Diane being there, and after a while she went very quiet of her own accord and sat in the kitchen, drinking Malvern water and shaking.

The bedroom he had made for himself and Pilar was the cause of her distress. Pelling had gone overboard with that in a big way. It was the kind of decor that only madmen or octogenarian art designers would contemplate: had Pilar been Dietrich herself it would have been over the top. A silk tent hung over the bed, which was itself raised on a plinth. Hideous purple tassels suggested the idea of a four poster. The sheets and pillows were black satin. The carpet was white. His clothes were next to a selection of her's in a long white wardrobe that ran the length of the room. On the short wall opposite the bed was a gilded Venetian mirror, six feet high and eight across. You looked on this room with real feelings of awe. If this was Pelling's idea of romance, he was out of his head, barking. There was a particularly ugly touch – on her side of the bed was a little white and gilt chair with her knickers and bra laid out just too, too casually for someone who had been shown the door months ago.

The adjoining bathroom was mirror tiled from floor to ceiling. There was a corner bath and in the space saved a fountain played in a miniature pool, the water dispensed by a naiad with a jug. He had not removed her scents and perfumes: maybe a hundred jars and bottles were shelved, all free of dust, all utterly redundant. He had made her a shrine, a tabernacle.

I found the room where she had first slept, when Melissa was still there and the fiction of her being his housekeeper had to be maintained. And I had a sudden flash of perception. I saw that Pilar had probably never occupied the master bedroom. He had spent thousands creating it as a true labour of love, but this room, tidy and sparsely furnished, was where she slept – and where he himself now laid down to weep. The bed had been occupied by a man and there was a bottle of Glenlivet on the floor. Scattered over the carpet were Polaroid photographs of her, some nude, some dressed to kill. The clothes she had not taken with her when she left were still in their drawers. There were a handful of early letters she had written to him on the London hotel stationery. Written in stilted English, they praised him for being a good man, expressed pleasure at his sweet nature and generosity. In a cupboard, her shoes were neatly racked, dozens of tiny pairs of them.

I poured myself a glass of his whisky and tidied up the Polaroids. For some reason I made the bed, even. I looked into the little shower room he had made for her when she first arrived. His disposable razors were scattered on the floor. His sleeping pills were on the glass shelf above the wash basin. In the waste bin were empty bottles of shampoo, coconut oil conditioner, shower gel. The towels were damp and dirty. The lady that cleaned for him never came up here. Blu-Tacked to the wall above the loo was a photograph of Pilar naked in a pool, maybe the hotel pool in London. She floated on her back, her arms straight back, the silver of the water mixing with her dark nipples and shadowed belly. By the trick of the flash, her eyes were redder than rubies. It was a terrible image for him to treasure. No matter what he thought he saw, to an outsider she was already gone. She wasn't really there at all. I left my whisky next to his sleeping tablets and went downstairs to his study.

"How much longer?" Diane asked, as I passed the kitchen.

"Two minutes."

"I didn't make him like this."

"Hush," I said. "I won't be long."

In the desk drawer there was the stage photograph of Melissa in her cardboard helmet, the one he had shown me what seemed aeons ago.

"Let's get out of here," Diane said from the doorway. I stood, and she walked towards me on stiff legs. Her expression was one of barely controlled agony. When we embraced, her whole body trembled. I held her tight to me, my arms bear-hugging her, my face in her hair.

"Go back to the cottage and pack a bag and your passport," I said. "Fill the car with petrol."

"I don't know that I can go through with this," she muttered.

"Yes, you can. This time you have to, Diane. It's something you have to do, or spend the rest of your life regretting. Be brave."

"I'm not brave."

"Meet me in half an hour. Say at the Salisbury. And don't stand me up."

When she had gone, I stayed sitting on his desk, staring mournfully at the room he had once considered to be all that life could offer in the way of luxury, before he met the woman to whom he could abase himself, not for a night, but forever. The little collections of this and that on the regency sofa tables, the select steel engravings on the walls: his earlier life in objects. And upstairs the monstrous cave of desire he had fashioned, the nightmare of his most elevated feelings, his homage to a whore. I felt, as tragedy teaches you to feel, pity and terror.

There was a photograph of the French house, tucked into a file of papers about its purchase and the bills for its renovation. I took the postcard Diane had given me when I got back from Carlisle and laid it down on his blotter, where he could not fail to find it. It was a view of a small castle called Neuviq-le-Chateau. On the reverse, a line or two from Melissa, saying she was safe and well.

I washed the glass Diane had used, turned off all the lights, double-checked the bolts on the back door and let myself into the mild and blowy night. Walking down to meet Diane, I passed a boy and his girl, kissing in the shadows of the pedestrian subway. His hands were inside her T-shirt, her lips were nuzzling his neck. She stood on tiptoe, pushing him back against the railings, oblivious to my footfall, her eyes closed ecstatically. For each of them, for that moment at least, the world had screeched to a halt. They were young, and it happened like that every time they kissed. Even in Hertford, it happened like that.

The hotel bed was higher than I was used to, and the morning light clearer. She lay face down, her arms by her side, her brown and newly slim back made darker by the whiteness of the sheets. It was a market day, and right under the window was a stall selling fish from the coast. I could hear amiable and unexcited conversation, and the singing of a bird in a cage across the little square. I kissed Diane's shadowed spine and held my palms out to the ceiling, where the sunshine danced, reflected back from the little puddles of overnight rain.

Somewhere in the hotel somebody was hoovering.

"This is heaven," Diane murmured.

I kissed her cool flesh again and stroked her hair away from her face.

"I didn't mean to wake you."

"I've been awake for hours."

She rolled over. The tan she'd got in Tenerife stopped where her bikini had begun. Two pale stripes accentuated her nakedness. She smiled at me with lazy good humour.

"Tell me this is heaven, Ganley."

"It's a principal ante-room of the same. The lobby. How did we get here? I can't even remember getting off the boat."

"I don't know where we are. I turned off an hour after we left the ferry. Don't fret. We can have this together, at least. Don't spoil it."

I swung my legs over the edge of the bed.

"I'm starving," I said.

Diane lay there, her arms folded above her head, one leg drawn up. Her expression had grown more serious. Her eyes searched mine.

"Later," she said. "You asked me to be brave, and I'm being brave. Don't tell me what you want to do any longer. It's what I want. I want this."

When my fingers touched her, she closed her eyes and turned her head towards the window and the light. She kicked the rumpled sheet away and opened her knees. Her arms reached out.

It was a little place called St Maur L'Eglise, and a furtive glance at the map showed we had many miles to go. Behind the church was a tiny esplanade that overlooked the river and the road south. We sat on a sun-warmed wall looking into the golden valley, our backs to England. Between us lay a bag of peaches.

"I will never ask you for another thing in your life," she promised. "Chance would be a fine thing, I know that. But I need this now. I need it for me. She'll survive. She's young. You and I are not so young. It means more."

"What does?"

She turned away without speaking.

So we played at tourists. We went inside the church and read the inscriptions of the memorial plaques. Down a side street we found a little museum of seashells and marine paintings donated to the commune by a crazy woman in the eighteen-fifties. Diane bought postcards. We had lunch at the Hotel du Commerce and slept it off down by the river, in the shade of a willow. Her blue singlet collected drifting white pollen; her bare arms and legs were dusted with it. She held onto my hand with a fierce grip, feigning sleep. But we could not afford to sleep for long. I rocked her gently with my free hand.

"Come on, Di. Be good."

"The only thing that's good to come out of this is you and me. I don't want to know everything there is to know, Patrick. I never did. I'm a dreamer. You hate me for that. But I don't want us to go any further. I want us to learn something about each other and forget the rest. Like this morning."

"This morning was the world on holiday."

"No," she sobbed.

"Look at me, Diane. I never expected to see you again.

When I did it was wonderful. You are wonderful. But we're here – here and now, I mean – because a man was killed."

"I don't care about that. I don't need a private detective. I don't want to set the record straight or bring the final curtain down. It can all go to hell."

"This is your daughter we're rushing off to find."

"And when we do, the problems will start all over again."

She sat up and threw herself into my arms, her breasts warm against my racing heart. Because, for a fraction of a second, I found myself agreeing: Melissa could go to hell. This way, her way, was some kind of escape. She stroked my face.

"I don't want us to go down there," she said. "Anywhere else but down there."

She took my hand and pulled it onto her breast, her lips against my protesting mouth. We rocked this way and that under the willows, Diane in a frenzy and exciting me into one too.

"Just take me away somewhere. Please. We'll go back to the hotel, rebook. We'll make love."

But the sheer madness of what we were doing down there while the rest of the countryside slumbered, was a sign of how impossible her wishes were. And she knew it. What had happened was not like a jigsaw that someone had clumsily knocked to the ground. The pieces would never go back as they were. It was like I said: we were there under the tree, kissing and tearing at each other because a man had been killed. And finally she pushed me away, her chest heaving, spit in her mouth. Her eyes were cloudy.

"God, how I hate her," she said. "I hate her for destroying thing so casually. Everything she touches breaks or goes rotten, smashes or blows up: and what happens to her? Nothing. She's the one person that'll come out of this still there, still unchipped."

197

"Let's get it over with."

"You're not listening," Diane shouted, beside her self with anger. "I want something good to happen to me!"

She jumped up and walked off a little way through the dappled sunshine. After a long minute or so, she began tucking in her singlet and straightening the waistband to her skirt. She held out her hand for me to throw her the sandals.

"Let's go and have a drink," I suggested.

"Oh yes! Let's be grown up about it."

"Di."

"Okay, I'm fooling myself thinking that I can depend on you. In the way that I want to depend. And I ought to be ashamed of myself for what I made when I made that kid. But it's all so bloody unfair. It's horrible how unfair it is."

"You don't have a choice."

"No? Supposing I say I'm not going on? It's my car, damn you."

"It's your daughter. If you take the car I'll go on by bus, or train, I don't know how. You know that's what I'll do. I can't help it. You can say it's vanity if you like. I'm vain enough to think it'll make a difference."

"You? You're so damn cynical you don't care what happens."

"You said something like that once before. And yet – how many times do you want me to say it? – here I am, here we are."

She hesitated, and then walked off across the meadow towards the walls of the town, her hands plunged into the pockets of her skirt, her shoulders high.

I lit a cigarette and threw some stones into the placid waters. She had left behind the sunglasses she had bought on the boat. I tried them on and the plastic hinge snapped on one of the supports. I could have kept on chucking stones into the river until I made an island, but what use was an island too small to live upon? So I threw the sunglasses instead.

When I walked up into the square, it was three and the patisserie, the chemist's and the hairdressers's salon were all opening up. Diane was waiting in the Tipo. She sat on the passenger side and did not look up when I opened the sizzling hot door. She had the road map on her lap.

We drove the rest of the afternoon: interminably to Tours, and then down the motorway to St Jean D'Angelys. It was a bad trip. If Melissa really was okay, as her card had said, we had come a long way for nothing very much. If she wasn't, neither of us was likely to be of the slightest bit of use anyway. Diane slept, and I only stopped myself from joining her by smoking like a damn beagle and playing tapes of Sinatra. In the end I don't know who I hated more – Melissa or Cole Porter.

"What are we going to do?" Di sulked when she woke. "Shouldn't we phone to say we're coming, so's she can plan something extra to screw up our lives?"

"Who's your favourite movie star?"

"Harry Dean Stanton."

"What would he do?"

"Oh God," she said, disgusted.

It was dark when we found the house. The gates were shut. No lights were on inside. I was so whacked from driving that I really didn't care any longer if the damn house suddenly upended and sank beneath the ground like the Titanic. We sat there staring at its silhouette, while half a mile away in the village, dogs barked and the kids circled around on their velos.

"What are we going to do, sit here all night?" Di demanded.

"No," a voice said from the shadows. "You're going to get out nice and slow and come inside."

"How are you, Denzil?" I asked.

"Very relaxed," he replied.

There was a pervasive smell of damp plaster in the house. Round the exterior walls was a little green tide mark. In the lobby of the house, Pelling had managed to save some of the beautiful original tiles, marmalade and toast in colour. But in the other ground floor rooms the floors had yet to be decided. Melissa – or perhaps Denzil – had made a table from a door. On it there were bowls of fruit and boxes of vegetables. The chairs were cheap supermarket camping equipment.

"Where is she?" Diane asked.

"My question to you. Your daughter ought to be in the pictures." He turned to me. "Nice to see you again, Mr Ganley."

There was nothing so crude as a gun in sight. Instead, Denzil turned out a tin of cassoulet for us, his bald head glistening under the naked light bulb. Guns weren't necessary. For some reason he had yet to explain, he was stark naked. This would make any other man vulnerable. Denzil looked as though he was weighing in for the WBO Middleweight Title.

"Has it been a hot day, Denzil?"

"I was in the bath. But yes, it's been warm. I don't wear a lot of clothes round the house anyway."

"How'd you get the scar on your belly?"

"An argument,' he said.

Diane sat down and put her head in her hands. But I was thirsty and fed up. I went to the fridge and pulled out a Kronenburg. Denzil smiled comfortably. He found a tape and shoved it into a battered ghetto-blaster.

"Don't do anything naff," he begged, leaving the room for a moment. When he came back he was wearing jeans.

"Eat, children. I've had mine. Sit down and scoff."

"Have you come to kill her?" Diane asked.

"Killing's a bit OTT," he said cheerfully. "I was just going to cut her nose off, or something like that."

"What has she done to you?"

"Don't be a nellie, Mrs Pelling. Eat your cassoulet."

So we ate, listening to Jim Morrison and the Doors, while Denzil sat peaceably reading an old copy of *Sud-Ouest*. Reading it, or just turning the pages. A dark shadow flitted across the wall.

"It's old Lenny the Lizard," Denzil said, without looking up.

Diane put her head down on the rough planks of the improvised table. From there she heard, as we all did, someone dragging open the gates and driving a car into the courtyard. I looked at Denzil. The gun hadn't been that far away after all: he had hidden it in the box of vegetables. Moving just as smooth and fast as Lenny, he held it now, nice and loose, his free arm folded across his chest.

"Not for her," he warned. "For you. Just don't do anything daft, Mr Ganley. You know what's wanted."

He moved away and stood in the shadows of the next room, as Pilar came into the room, looking vexed and thirsty, but radiant in a white cotton T-shirt and blue-black harem trousers.

SIXTEEN

"Right. You," Pilar said, pointing at Diane, "can clear off anytime you like. You go back with Denzil. You can have a shower if you like, but then you get out of here. I just can't be bothered to deal with you."

"Just a minute," Diane said, jumping up.

Pilar studied her briefly.

"You've lost weight," she said. "And not before time. Whose idea was it to drag you down here? Ganley's? I bet you didn't want to come. Well, you were right. Fat or thin, you're in the way. You're out of it. If you give Denzil any trouble he'll break your back."

"Take it easy, princess," Denzil murmured. Pilar waved him away and pointed at me.

"This one," she said, "stays with me. We stay here until that daft bitch turns up from wherever she's hiding, we talk, I poke her eyes out with a bread knife or something, and then he takes me home."

"Let me guess, Pilar. You're feeling pretty pissed off all round," I suggested.

"I ought to have got your legs and arms broken long ago. There's only one more stupid person in the world and that's her husband. You think you're looking at Bob Westerman's killer, don't you? You've got it all worked out. That's what's running around London. Even this useless cow here thinks I killed Bob. Or had him killed. And that would be to avenge poor little Melissa, I suppose. You people are unbelievable."

"Sit down, Pilar," Denzil said. "Let me mix you a drink."

"I ought to shoot your eyes out!" Pilar shouted at me. "I told you, months and months ago, to mind your own business."

She sat down next to Diane and put her head in her hands. Denzil tucked the gun in his waistband. He was smiling, but there was no happiness there.

"I'll do it," I said.

"Bacardi and coke. With ice."

"My God," Pilar said through laced fingers. "I must have been mad."

It was one of those gnomic remarks it is far better not to pursue in any detail. But I did have a flash image of her the day she dimpled prettily and said yes to the gangling Tony Pelling, awkward on the hotel bedroom carpet. It had been one big disaster for her from that moment on.

"Go and have that shower," Denzil advised Diane. "If the lady wants you out, you're out."

"You think I'm going to get into a car with you?"

"Yes," Denzil said.

I followed her into the bathroom, partly to keep her company, and partly to try and wake up. While she shivered and shrank in the shower, I ran cold water over my neck and wrists and chased a startled millipede around the untiled floor. Things were not exactly going to plan. Apart from the doubtful benefit of a plate of tinned cassoulet each, we had nothing much to feel good about. True, there was a window in the bathroom that gave onto a grassy farm track and so, round the side of the house, to the road and the car. Unfortunately, Denzil had the keys to the Tipo. I did not fancy running around the sunflowers at eleven at night with a distraught Diane, chased by the incandescant Pilar. I'd end up like the millipede, cowering in the corner.

"What are we going to do?" she whispered, as I patted her dry with the towel.

"I don't know."

"You don't *know*?"

"What do you want me to say, Diane? That is one very narked woman out there."

Naked, she opened the window and stuck her upper half out. It was a bad time for Pilar to come in. Her smile was thin.

"Get your big bum back in here, Mumsie, and get in that other room."

"Who do you think you are talking to, you skinny whore?" Pilar's smile evaporated.

"She's coming," I said.

We rejoined them in the middle of a fraught silence. Denzil had resumed his study of the newspaper and Pilar was pouring herself the kind of drink that would stun an elephant. The gun was on the table, but I had already decided against doing anything heroic with it. I hoped Diane felt the same way. Pilar pointed a finger at us. She was in a very gestural mood.

"First of all, your husband is the biggest creep in the whole world. That is for starters. Secondly, your daughter needs some kind of brain transplant. She needs something bigger than the brains of a gnat she was born with. I am an extremely cautious person, Mrs Pelling. I don't get excited. And I'm not evil. I may not be good, but I'm not wicked. I'm careful. But tonight I could kill you all."

"Where is Melissa?" I asked.

"You tell me," Pilar said.

"You haven't found her?"

"Does it look as though I've found her?"

Silence. And a very tense silence, too. It seemed to infuriate Pilar. She banged the table with her fist.

"One knee in the groin would have stopped Westerman. I don't know what shit Tony'd fed you, but Westerman was about as determined as—" (she waved her arms about) "—a lettuce. He was a filthy rat of a human being, a disgusting man, but he could have been stopped. Any other girl would have kicked his balls up inside him."

"This is the feminist in you speaking, is it?"

"You shut up," she advised me. "You watch your mouth. What he did was rape, and he had to be punished for it. But that girl, she could have fought him."

"She says she did."

Pilar nodded at me slowly. I found it hard to hold her eyeline. In matters like this, she was coming from a long, long way back. We were talking the difference between the shanty towns of the Manilan suburbs, where a child screaming in her uncle's house or running down the street away from her grandfather was just another sound in the night, and Hertford. She leaned across the table and took one of my cigarettes, her eyes still firmly on me. I looked down at my hands, ashamed. Denzil tried to pour a little oil on troubled waters.

"The kid has been causing problems with threats and wild words," he said gently. "She's just a kid, but she ought to know better by now."

"What threats? What has she got to threaten you with?"

"Don't act dumb," Pilar said. "Melissa thinks she understands things. She thinks she knows how the world works."

"She thinks you killed him. And Tony Pelling also thinks you did it."

205

"Tony Pelling is a pathetic creep. He should have stayed with Tubby here. The three of them deserve each other. Westerman asked to be killed – he had it coming to him. The French think he was mugged and robbed. That's good enough for me. He's dead, and the world is a better place without him. Lots of people die every second of the day who are worth ten of him."

"Then leave us alone!" Diane shouted.

Pilar put her hands either side of the older woman's face, and pulled her forward until their noses almost touched.

"Listen, you dopey bitch. Nothing would give me greater pleasure. Your daughter and your husband between them have wrecked my life. *You* ducked out, remember? *I* was prepared to take them on. I must have been crazy, but that's what I wanted. Now every second-rate genius in London thinks I killed the Canadian."

"Has she gone to the police?" I asked.

"If she has, we're all in trouble. But has it occurred to you, big-shot, that *she* killed the bastard?"

It had. Diane was looking aghast, but Pilar looked at me with such anger in her eyes that I was forced to conclude that she was either a consummate actress, or she had a real bone to pick with Melissa.

"My daughter couldn't do a thing like that," Diane said, shaky.

"Your daughter thinks she's smarter than any of us. Westerman did her wrong. And why didn't she come straight home and rat on him? Because Daddy was his friend. You discover that she's pregnant – and what do you do about it? Nothing. You promise not to tell. Everything that's happened to her started when you took her on holiday."

"No," Diane sobbed.

"Yes. You asked her who it was and she wouldn't tell.

206

Tony asked her and she wouldn't tell. Who do you think did all the guessing? Me. So I tell Tony. But that won't do it either. Bob was his friend, there had to be some mistake. He swears me to silence. So now we all know who did it to her and nobody's saying a thing."

"Who called in Roskill?" I asked gently.

Pilar glanced.

"I did. I thought it could be sorted out privately."

"What about Denzil? Wouldn't he have been a better bet?"

"I never liked him," Denzil admitted. "It would have been a pleasure to sort him out. But the princess chose differently."

"Roskill had enough on him to keep him out of England forever. That was the plan. I wanted him to sweat. I wanted him to live in dread that Charlie Roskill's tapes and videos would one day drop through the mail at his rotten university. Denzil would have maimed or killed him, if I'd asked. But I didn't want that. I wanted him to live with the sweat running down his ribs every time anyone in Canada even mentioned England."

"And then Pelling arranged to meet him here."

"Mr Dreamboat took a hand, yes."

"He was going to warn him."

"Maybe," Pilar said. "Maybe he was going to say how sorry he was it had all come unstuck, their lovely friendship. Maybe he was going to apologise to Bob. You know, for Melissa letting herself get raped and spoiling everything."

"That's too bitter, Pilar."

"You think so?"

Pilar turned a baleful eye on Diane.

"Don't get any ideas, Mrs Pelling. What I did for your kid was done to protect myself. Your husband was my ticket out of all this stuff. I've lived with shit in my mouth since I was nine years old. What you gave up in Hertford doesn't seem

207

very much to you. But it was all I needed. I had plans for your husband. Or his money, anyway. You can live like a slut if you want. I've been there. I don't want it anymore."

"Why did you make him bring Melissa with him?' I asked.

"To remind him. He's weak. He's stupid. Westerman could run rings round him. I thought the girl would keep him straight."

We sat round the table as our more fractious French neighbours might sit discussing pigs or goats, or a disputed parcel of land. Overhead, huge moths whacked into the light bulb and dropped to the floor like toffee papers. It was too surreal for words. The gun lay between us, but nobody seemed to notice it. I was so tired all I could fret about was when we could all go to bed, and how we would sleep. All four of us were smoking cigarettes like the last people to do so left in Europe. Pilar sat with silent tears running down her face.

"I have known some real bastards in my time," she said. "I thought your lot were different. They're worse. They're incompetent bastards. This is what you get when you believe what punters tell you."

"Did you kill him, Pilar?"

"What's the difference," she said, bleak. "He's dead."

Diane and I slept in the grenier, on an inflatable double mattress. We did not undress. I fell asleep listening to Pilar and Denzil talking. Their voices rose and fell like waves out to sea. Every so often the fridge door clinked open. Once in a while I could hear her crying. Diane lay on her back, her arm across her face, snoring. I rolled her over and she went into the swimmer's position, like someone diving down through the waters of a reef, her hands lax, but her toes pointed.

I woke again about four. There was that unmistakable whispering silence downstairs, that charged secrecy of the dark, broken by rustles and sweet nothings that told me they were making love.

"Not yet, not yet," Pilar breathed, immediately beneath me in the room below. I lay staring at the new roof beams Pelling had caused his builder to install, lit by a midsummer moon.

Downstairs, her whispered sigh came like the cry of something wounded. A little after that, the first birds began to squabble in the eaves. I lay staring at the massive beams until my eyes began to ache, while beside me Diane slept on, her clothes stuck to her body with sweat.

When I woke again, the sun was coming through the little square windows of the grenier and Diane was in the shower. Downstairs, Radio France Musique was smoothing out the wrinkles and the whistling kettle was doing its duty.

I came down and walked into the cluttered and dank smelling salle de séjour. It was empty. I unlocked the door and opened the windows and the shutters. Their car had gone, and so had they.

"Maybe for bread, or croissants," Diane suggested nervously. We waited. After an hour, when they had yet to return, Diane seemed to relax. She sat in the sun with a cup of coffee on her knee, her eyes closed against the sunshine. Dour men in tractors passed, not without staring in at us. The jasmine that clung to the house was ruffled by a faint breeze. Len the Lizard came out to warm himself, hanging preposterously on the glinty grey limestone.

"They've gone for good," Diane said, triumphant. "You've scared them off."

"That was clever of me. I remember it all being the other way round. She scares me shitless."

"She's just a bad loser," Diane said, making me wonder which planet she had been born on. She went upstairs, dragged down the double lilo, took her clothes off and sunbathed. I sat inside the house, sulking and chain smoking. If Diane had her way, we would stay here eating tuna salad and drinking Bordeaux until the pale stripes left by her Tenerife bikini changed colour and her flesh was one gorgeous brown. She had even brought her suntan oil. It was a bad experience, that morning after the night before. None of us seemed to be on the same page.

"Where are you going?" she asked.

"I'm going out for a primal scream somewhere. If I can find someone smaller than me, and older, I might kick them. I'm just going out. I may be some time."

"Buy some cheese and bread," she murmured, the sun tan lotion glistening cheerfully on her rump. "Don't buy meat. I'll shop for us later. And don't sit around drinking all day."

"Don't *you* sprain your brain or anything silly like that. And do give the guys who are going past on tractors a full eyeful. They don't get a lot of laughs."

She rolled over onto her back and lay there glowering. But I was in no mood to be glowered at. I walked to the Tipo, dusty and warm, and decorated with wisps of hay. Tucked under the windscreen wiper was a scrap of green paper torn from a flyer about a bal musette. On the free space, scribbled in pencil, was the name of a village or town. The handwriting was that of the student of Bismarck – a little freer, a little more slapdash, but with the same silly a's and e's. Good. I had a map, I had a day to find her, and when I did, I had someone to kick.

SEVENTEEN

Like her mother, Melissa was doing some serious sunbathing. I found her in the garden of a M. Delcasse, an elderly and suave Parisian who was enjoying the more contemplative side to life after a career in economic journalism. These were his exact words, delivered in painfully correct English, as we waited for Melissa to go inside and put some clothes on. Delcasse, as he went on to explain, was teaching her French – already quite good, but lacking that certain something that marks out the idiomatic speaker.

"What's she teaching you?" I asked.

Delcasse smiled. He was completely imperturbable, as befitted a man who lived in an eighteenth century house overlooking a twelfth century church. His gardener worked in the gravelled courtyard, his house was filled with books and pictures, his Audi with the Paris plates glittered in the road outside. He wore his pullover tied round his neck, had his slacks made for him somewhere or other by a devoted tailor, and his hair was so beautifully cut it made you wince with envy.

"I find the English very sympathetic," he murmured. "You

know, so much of life today is complex, people's motives are so nuanced. Melissa is refreshingly simple to understand. It's like watching bad television. Or reading the comic papers."

"Beautifully put, M. Delcasse."

"I would say she has a lot to learn, were it not for the fact that she is practically ineducable. I do hope you've come to take her away."

"You won't miss her?"

"It has been a strain on what I pride myself is normally an hospitable nature."

"You won't miss the peep show of firm young flesh?"

"I think I *am* supposed to appreciate that," he admitted. "But I draw you back once again to the notion of the un-nuanced. All other personal preferences aside, I think some mysteries are worth preserving. The gardener will be sorry to see her go, of course."

He brushed a little dust from his slacks and smiled again, only this time a little shorter, a little more privately.

"He's all right," Melissa said as we drove off. "I only met him the other day. He's waiting for his boyfriend to come back from Italy or something. Is Pilar really angry?"

"Yes," I said. "Does that bother you?"

"I don't want to face her just at the moment."

"Well, that's great. I'll pass that along when I see her, shall I? And do up the buttons on your blouse."

She stuck her tongue out at me.

"What an old misery-guts you are."

"Pilar, can I remind you, is talking about poking your eyes out."

"For what?"

"For an unjust accusation of murder. That's *murder*, Melissa, as in killing someone else."

"I'm not afraid of Pilar."

"Of course not. That's why you're hiding out with old Smoothy-boots."

"I am not hiding out."

She was jumpy, but trying to disguise it.

"Where are we going?"

"Back to your mother. She's waiting at the house."

"Not just yet," she said, laying a brown hand on my forearm. The gesture was unmistakable. I looked at her sharply.

"This is me, remember?"

"Turn left here – à gauche! you can buy me a drink."

We pootled along for another kilometre or so and came to the Café Maroc, a drunk of a place leaning against its neighbour, a garage, at a sleepy little crossroads. It offered a couple of dusty benches and a table in the full glare of the sun. Melissa immediately sat down and hitched up her sarong-style skirt. She leaned back luxuriously.

"You look white and English," she said.

"You look English and smug."

A sour old man with a wall eye came out to serve us. She asked for a Suze and I ordered a beer.

"Now I hope we're not going to have a scene," she said.

"Melissa, I have something to say to you: for a glorious few months you have waded through deep shit and come out smelling of bath essence. But this is real now. This is heavy duty danger you're in."

"What danger? Look around you, Ganley. We're in la belle France. This is one of the hidden beauties of Charente. I'm going to stay here all summer. I'm going to find myself. I've had it with London."

"Who killed Westerman?" I asked, as brutally as I could.

She flinched, but only for an instant, and only out of exasperation.

"That's all been looked after by the French police."

213

"This is a new position of yours, is it? An idea that's come to you recently?"

She looked surprised.

"No, I've always thought that."

"Then why is Pilar so mad with you?"

She took one of my cigarettes and held it in her fingers, unlit. I realised something about her I had never thought before: she was in a movie of her own life. She was playing a girl called Melissa who's taken her pitcher to the well. All these little touches – the tan, the gold chain round her wrist, the cigarette as a prop, the wacky location – were part of a screen version of herself. When I took the cigarette away Melissa pouted. A car passed, blowing her wrap around skirt open even more. It was all in the script.

"I asked you a question. Why is Pilar mad?"

"Maybe she killed him," she said at last.

"Who have you shared that sweet thought with?"

"What difference does it make to you?"

Melissa the gamine. Melissa the crazy girl with a crazy story to tell, who has fallen into the habit of bragging, and can't tell the simplest lie without icing and marzipan.

"Charlie Roskill was shot dead four days ago."

This hit her, and she looked down into her Suze.

"I'm sorry to hear that."

"And?"

"What else do you want me to say? I'm sorry, that's all."

I reached across the American cloth of the table and slapped her hard on the cheek. Some of the Suze spilled onto her bare thigh and ran round the packed muscle.

"I want you to say something that shows you can talk like a grown up if you want to. It's all going to come out in court, Melissa. We're not in a book or a film. And it's not any longer a story about you. Three people are dead. All murdered. You

214

seem to have fingered Pilar for one of them."

"Yes, well," she shouted. "Would any of this have happened if they had stayed together the way other people do? Or at any rate pretended? Isn't that what most people do?"

She meant her parents. She snatched back her cigarette and lit it from the box of matches in front of us.

"Did I ask for any of this to happen? You probably met Sid, at the *Blue Skies*. It's the sort of thing you like, tracking people down. He and his wife were wonderful to me, really great. I was very unhappy and a bit mad, I suppose. I thought Sid would try to feel me up, I took it for granted he would take the opportunity. Maybe I wanted it, even. 'Keep your hand on your ha'penny, Mels' was as far as he ever got. That and a pat on the back as the train came in."

"There are plenty of people like him," I said. "There's plenty of goodness in the world."

"You *would* know that," she scoffed. "What do you do except go round eating out of other people's dustbins?"

The patron of the café had come out to lean against the door frame and watch us. Melissa glanced at him, and some sense of reality seemed to register with her. She looked at me, though, with defiance.

"Pilar is capable of anything."

"Your father thinks she's terrific."

She held up her hand to stop me going on, her eyes glittering.

"I was raped, Ganley. I was buggered on my hands and knees in some ditch. And I was told it was what I needed. That I was asking for it. We didn't know anybody like that until Pilar came along."

"So why did she kill Westerman?"

"I don't know," Melissa said after a pause.

I reached and took her hand. Maybe this was in the script

215

too, but I felt sorry for her, with her quivering lower lip and wet lashes. She was an impressive looking child, but she was, after all, only a child.

"I shouldn't have slapped you," I said. "Pilar didn't bring Westerman into the house: your father did. And you must have half suspected that. Otherwise you'd have run home and told him. You'd have told your ma. But you could see that something was happening between your dad and the Canadian. Now tell me something – and I want an honest answer, Melissa."

"Go ahead," she muttered. "What do I care?"

"Your father brought you to France last year. He had some business with the builders and he took you along. Did you know he was going to meet Westerman?"

"We went to Angoulême to meet him off the Paris train," she said scornfully.

"But when you set out from Hertford, did you know?"

"No," she said, after a while.

"When did you know?"

"On the way down there."

"He just mentioned it."

"Yes."

"So, after you'd arrived, a night or so after, he said 'Well now, Mels darling, shall we go and pick up Bob?'"

"Yes."

"Good," I said.

"What does that mean?"

"It means I don't believe you."

I'd got her back in the car, but now it was my turn to procrastinate. I had absolutely no desire to return her to Diane, because I knew that within five minutes their mutual gift for self-deception would engage and interlock, there would be

216

exclamations about suntans and weight loss, hair gels and nail varnish, and we'd be back where we started. For her part, Melissa was sulking up a storm. It was extremely hot and the sweat was running down her face and neck. When we came to an arrosage, a huge jet of white spray playing across the fields of sunflowers, she asked me to stop. She walked across the pebbly verge and stood directly in the path of the spray.

"It doesn't matter who killed him. He's dead," she shouted.

"That's the historian in you speaking, is it?"

"You're such a creep. What are you trying to do, Ganley, save my soul? You think I can come out of this somehow without suffering and be a nice wifie to someone in five or ten years time? With a fucking *degree*?"

The huge feathery spray swept to and fro over her head in a thirty degree arc. She was soon drenched to the skin, her clothes pasted to her, her hair in rats tails.

"*I* killed him! It was *me*! Does that make you happy?"

And she threw herself onto the ground, sobbing. I ran to the edge of the field and pulled her to her feet. Her face, her shoulders, were covered in reddish mud. I put my arms round her and half-dragged, half-lifted her clear of the spray. The sun beat down on us, but she shook like someone dragged from the winter ice.

"It's okay, it's okay," I said.

"What is?" she shouted wildly. "Killing him?"

"You didn't."

She screamed and ran away up the road, losing a sandal, falling over on the chaussée, getting up again and stumbling on. I walked slowly after her, leaving the car with the doors wide open. After a hundred metres she fell to her knees. For the second time I pulled her to her feet, and this time carried her back to the Tipo. I drove with her curled up, arms round

217

her knees, as I had seen her father behave in the Carlisle motel.

"Don't take me back there," she whispered.

This part of France was once at the edge of the English dominions, in the days when men hunted through the woods for deer and boar; and on occasions, each other. But long before that, the Romans had garrisoned the gentle uplands, so that startled English soldiers foraging for food and women would come across amphitheatres deep in the forests, apparently in the middle of nowhere. And that is what we did. We sat in the buzzing half shade of a clearing and looked down on a semi-circle hacked into the side of a hill. The seats, the ruins of the dressing rooms, were all still there, only covered with grass and brambles. It was a find, because although it had been signposted for five kilometres, nothing had been added or taken away. It was just a set of old stones in thick woodland.

Melissa wore a sweater from the back of the car while her clothes hung on branches, dripping dry. She lay on her side, her hands to her face, her knees drawn up.

"What is in all this for you?" she asked.

"I don't know. Your mother, perhaps."

"You know that's pure bullshit."

"Think so?"

"You could go away and live your own life. Get a job, settle down. Stay inside yourself. You were a policeman, weren't you?"

"I was in the police," I amended.

"You can't change anything. You can't make it stop, or go away. You can't turn it round. Its' just cheap thrills for you. That's why people do your job."

"Maybe," I said. "And maybe there's more to it than that."

But this was her other voice, and I liked it better. All the provocation of the little scene in the Café Maroc was gone.

She rolled over, dragging the hem of the sweater down for modesty and looking me in the eye.

"Westerman was soft. You imagine rapists to be hard. But he was flabby. Not just physically, but every way. He was just slime. There were girls at school—"

She hesitated.

"Talk," I said.

"There were stories. You'd have liked that. They came in after the weekend and things had happened. In cars, in bed, with flowers, with pools of vomit. I used to wonder about it. But I was always on the outside. I was put on the outside by the rest of them. For being fat, obviously. And a swot. And dim. At the same time as being a swot, dim."

"Didn't you have any friends?"

"Once," she said. "When I was younger. But much younger. Westerman asked me the same sort of questions. He was very – what's the word I want? Solicitous."

"Who are you going to trust, Melissa?"

She glanced at me, before jumping up and retrieving her blouse and skirt from their branches.

"He told me I asked for it. Afterwards. When he made me clean myself up. He said I could have stopped it. It was my fault, for having the suitable holes in my body. And he was so afraid, so weak, that I believed him. I was bleeding onto his car seat, it was all too late, and still I believed him. Not that it was my fault, but that I *could* have stopped him. He even asked me why I wasn't crying."

"Enough."

"Isn't this what you want to hear?"

She turned her back on me and pulled off the sweater. I walked to the other side of the clearing while she dressed. A couple of young women walking down below looked up in interest. From their point of view, something very different to what was actually happening was in progress. Melissa came up behind me.

"Let's walk," I said.

There was a track wide enough to pass along side by side: I put my arm round her and we ambled slowly along the ridge, breaking apart now and then to duck branches or skip brambles.

"You stink of tobacco," Melissa said.

"Tobacco and old books. I don't have any old books, but that's my style."

"My mother's gone for you in a big way, I suppose?"

"Your mother's affairs are private. Are we going to walk all the way to Poitiers, or are we going to turn back?"

"She likes me to call her Diane. She likes the idea that we're closer now, because of what happened. I am supposed to be strong, stronger than her. I'm supposed to get over it."

"That's going to be difficult for everybody."

"Oh good," she said bitterly. "I feel better already."

She broke loose and walked off downhill. I followed, passing the two French girls climbing up, hand in hand, and giving me a knowing glance. The trees gradually thinned out, and I caught up with Melissa by the side of a field. From here, the landscape rolled back, field upon field, valley upon valley, to a lavender coloured horizon more than twenty miles away. She sat watching it, crying.

"Can't you leave me alone?"

"Come on, Mels. I'm not hounding you. This time, you ran away to where you knew everyone could find you. It has to end some time. You've done enough."

She turned to me with bleary eyes.

"I planned a hundred different ways of killing him. Or having him die. Of burying him here, say, where he could just rot to nothing."

"But you didn't kill him, did you? It didn't work out like that."

She put her head on her plump knees and sobbed. I stroked her back, feeling choked and horribly male, horribly capable of causing this grief just because I was male. In that moment, of touching her, of moving my hand from her back to her neck, I felt enough contamination from what Westerman had done to her to want to kill him myself. But I had to persist.

"He came to the house, didn't he? You met him off the train in Angoulême, both of you, and he came to the house."

"You're so bloody clever, you tell me."

"I think he did."

She picked up a twig and pressed it into the flesh of her arm. It was too blunt to pierce her but she pressed until it snapped.

"The thing you have to realise is that for a long time I felt the shame he should have had. I was guilty for both of us."

"And your dad? Did you shoulder his guilt too?"

She shook her head to stop me from going on.

"I don't want to talk about it. It's all useless anyway. Something happened. A lot of things happened. It was like a dream."

Walking back towards the car she volunteered her firm dry hand. We must have looked like lovers. She pulled to a stop and kissed me briefly on the cheek.

"I know you want to be kind."

"I want you to be kind to yourself."

We kissed each other on the lips. It was a form of parting. Melissa walked on. When the two girls we had seen earlier bumped down the track in their little Peugeot, waving good-bye, she turned and waited for me, dust swirling in the sunbeams.

"Working for Roskill was a dumb thing to do. It was a way

of punishing myself. Zach, even, was a way of hurting myself. Some of the girls I was at school with are engaged to be married. Can you *believe* that? I met a girl who's doing modern languages at Cambridge – we bumped into each other in Covent Garden. So we had lunch. This girl has found true love. It's all she wanted to talk about. I was supposed to fill in the rest: the sex, the bonking as she'd call it. And while we talked she was eyeing me up and down. I wasn't as envious as she would have liked. She asked me if I was a lesbian."

"There we are. That's higher education for you."

She laughed in spite of herself, and wiped the tears from her cheeks with the back of her hand.

"What am I going to do, Ganley?"

"Well, you could practise calling me Patrick. We could meet here every year and have an anniversary picnic. I could tell you *my* sad story. You could run away some more until you bring everybody to their knees with exhaustion. Any of those things. Or we could have one more drink, go home and face the music."

"Let's have one more drink."

EIGHTEEN

There was no one at the house, where the doors and windows were open in that reckless English way that scandalises the continent. The blue lilo mattress was in the courtyard, the suntan bottle open by its side. The radio was playing and the kettle on the camping stove was warm. There was a tea without milk on the improvised table. The clothes Diane had worn the previous day were drying on a line strung between two posts of the old cow byre. But of Diane herself, there was no trace.

"She's gone for a walk," Melissa said, disgusted. "In her sun outfit, I bet. That woman's a natural tourist."

"Make some tea," I suggested. When she went inside, I wandered round the barns, trying not to look or act methodical.

"There's all kind of junk in there," Melissa called.

I pushed past rolls of chicken mesh, stacked boxes and crates. There were hundreds of bottles sacked up in fertiliser bags and pallets of tiles as high as a man. There were farm carts and ancient bicycles, rotten straw and forty gallon drums. And every so often, like a fairy tale, little stars of blood in the dust.

"What is it?" Melissa asked at my elbow, making me jump.

"Go back into the house."

"What's happened?"

"Do as you're told."

There was a small wicket gate at the corner of one barn, secured by a wooden gate bleached grey by the sun. It was open. The aperture framed a vignette of green and gold countryside bathed in blinding sunlight. I screwed up my eyes. Sitting against the wall on the inside, in the dark of the barn, was a familiar figure, hugging her bloodied chest.

"You took your time," she said.

"Jesus! Where's Denzil?"

"It was my bright idea to handle things my way. The woman's way. Denzil's playing pool with the boys in Ruffec."

"Can you stand? Have you broken anything?"

"Help me up, can you?" Pilar asked, holding out her skinny arms. But before I could reach for her, she rolled over onto her hip in a dead faint.

We dragged the mattress back indoors and laid her down on it. The blood was coming from a deep black gash in her shoulder and gravel-filled grazes to her chest and hip; but the real pain was located in cracked, maybe broken ribs. Melissa knelt beside her enemy and bathed the cuts. She was very good, very calm and efficient. She had me tear up a T-shirt of Diane's to make swabs. Pilar found it funny, in a shocked hysterical sort of way. Little pearls of water ran down and collected in her belly button, only to be shaken out by her agonised laughter.

"What the hell did he hit you with?"

"He ran me over, the bastard. He's a crap driver, of course."

"Who is?" Melissa asked, her lips tight and straight.

224

"Your father. The old goat has at last got up a head of steam. He came in here like gang-busters and ran me down. I don't think it was an accident. Your ma and I were standing out there talking – and wham! Maybe it was all too much for him."

"He aimed the car at you?"

"He ran me down. I didn't go under the wheels and he tried to reverse and do better. Diane got him out of the car."

"Then what?"

"It wasn't popular. He chased her in here and I hid in the barns."

"She's in shock," Melissa muttered.

"No I'm not. Let Ganley do his number on me. Go on, Ganley. Ask me more."

I picked up her hand and held it. Her grip was far too tight.

"What happened, after Diane ran in here?"

"Lots of bumping and crashing. Then he dragged her out by her hair and chucked her in the car."

"Was he drunk?"

Pilar laughed and winced her way through that one. I thought of something else.

"Where's your car?"

"Exactly. Denzil dropped me off. He didn't want to, but I knew better. Great. He's coming back for me at six. You better do something brave and resourceful, big-shot. Otherwise, Mr Pelling's a dead man."

I looked down at her, bruised and bloodied, naked save for her lemon yellow knickers and torn white skirt, and nodded. Denzil would take all this unkindly.

"She should see a doctor," Melissa said.

"I think you'll need some help with Denzil first," Pilar said, trying to laugh and groaning instead. Her stomach muscles were tight as ropes. I stroked her forehead. It was wet

225

with sweat. Melissa jumped up and ran from the room. We could hear her footfall in the grenier as she charged about, making ancient dust fall on our heads. Pilar smiled. In an involuntary gesture I kissed her hand, still joined to mine in a fierce grip. She smiled some more, but looking vague.

"He's flipped," she whispered. "Maybe he's drunk too, but I think he's really gone."

"What does he want with Diane?"

"She was great. She stopped him from following me and beating me to death. We had a tense five minutes here, I can tell you. The poor bastard is out of his skull."

Melissa arrived with a sheet and a duvet. She pushed me out of the way and laid the sheet reverently over Pilar's naked-ness. The effect was macabre. Pelling's former mistress peered out over the hem of the sheet, looking very ill indeed.

"Go to a phone or something and get a doctor," Melissa said, tears in her eyes.

"I'm not too keen on leaving you."

"He's my father, for heaven' sake."

Pilar actually tried to chuckle.

"Poor old Ganley," she wheezed.

A shadow fell across the threshold and I wheeled round. Diane stood there, dressed, uninjured, apparently unharmed in any way, but her shoulders slumped.

"He wants to see you," she said in a flat, broken voice.

"Are you all right?"

"He's waiting in the car."

I stood up slowly Diane looked at me with an expression of such resignation, such emptiness, that I knew we were lost to each other forever. I knew then what she knew. Her eyes swept over me once more and then extinguished themselves.

"Can you take charge here?"

226

"Just don't hurt him," she said, ignoring the question and sitting on one of the camp chairs as if waiting for the doctor. Her hands were in her lap, and she looked down at them like someone with time to kill.

"I'll come too," Melissa said.

"No you won't," her mother said absently. "You'll stay here."

"Drive," he said.

"Where?"

"It's been a field day for you, hasn't it? Just drive, I'll tell you where."

He looked blotchy. He looked – and it was an achievement – he looked dangerous. He wore slacks and a white and blue striped shirt, and on his head was an umpire's straw trilby. Cloudy grey sweat ran down his face and he shook like someone in a fever. He was no less a stick insect, no less pathetically gawky, but what was coming out of him was a burning heat, the wildness of fire when it leaves the domesticated hearth and begins to eat the house. It was a horrible image, because on his lap was the green plastic spare petrol can, and half the contents were over his legs and swilling around on the floor. I wound back the sunroof and felt about as practical as Canute.

"It's going to go up, Tony. With or without your help it's going to blow. This is very, very dangerous."

He opened his hand and showed me the disposable lighter.

"Start the car," he said.

I looked at the position of his thumb on the little green slip of plastic, looked at the ignition key in the steering column, looked at the road in front of us and thought, for only the second time in my life: *well, this is it*.

"Start the engine," Pelling said.

227

"You don't want to say goodbye?"

He jerked the neck of the can at me. The slops hit me in the chest.

I turned the key with shaking fingers – and nothing happened. Nothing happened save the agonised roar of the engine and a warm stain between my legs as my bladder took over from my mind. I pulled away, driving like some schoolboy taking his test.

"I am terrified," someone said. It was me. There was a clatter as he threw the can out of his window. I hardly registered that. The road unreeled in front of us – little trees, big trees, falling down barns, barns with massive harvesters inside. The petrol was biting my chest.

"I could kill you for what you have done to us," Pelling said, as if plucking a remote theoretical possibility out of the air, or loosing a bow at a venture.

"Good," I heard myself saying. I was driving round bends and through little patches of shade with exaggerated care and attention. The sun beat down mercilessly. I could not say I had a plan – I had an image of his daughter standing under the irrigation spray, her clothes plastered to her, her brown body shining through. I was trying to call over this spray from wherever the hell we had found it, make it lope across the rolling fields and drench us. It was like wanting to believe in God.

"Turn left," he said.

We bumped along a narrow metalled track towards a telecommunication tower with a red band painted round it a hundred feet up. It looked horribly like a giant match. But this is good, I thought. He's going to make me get out of the car and climb the stairs – they must have stairs inside – and jump from the top. Jumping a hundred and twenty feet onto six inches of topsoil is a good bet. Those are good odds.

The tower passed on our right. We drove downhill and through a sleeping village. Please don't come out to wave. Please don't strike any matches or grind any knives or scissors. My eyes were smarting from the petrol vapour. The road that left the village forked.

"Take the right," he said.

"Sure?"

"Don't make me do it, Ganley."

And I loved him for that. Petrol in my shirt, piss running down my legs, I loved him as warmly as any son for the possibility that he was actually in two minds about killing us both. I had not looked at him once since we started. He filled his side of the car like a dark giant, a fog, a mountain. Little snatches of the actual, that he was a skinny beanpole wearing a silly hat, a classic nerd of an Englishman abroad, flitted through my mind like dreams.

"Stop here."

We drew up in a dip, where the road traversed a little wooded ravine. I forced myself to look at him. He held the lighter up in front of his face, thumb at the ready. His mouth was wet. Strands of his hair poked down from the brim of his hat and were plastered to his long sloping forehead by sweat. The more ridiculous, the more terrifying. I turned off the ignition, waiting for the *whoomp* that would come from some errant spark under the dashboard. Nothing, except a flash from Pelling's glasses as they caught the sun. I found that my shoulders were aching with tension, and forced myself to relax. My legs were trembling like jellies.

"This is where I killed him," he said calmly. "I didn't think I could do it, but it had to be done."

He looked round about him with his habitual peering insistence on accurate accounting.

"I think this is the place," he said.

229

"Why don't we get out and check?"

He held the lighter in front of my face.

"He was like you, in many ways. I was seduced by him to begin with. Oh yes. He had a story to tell – he had a hundred stories. But he was shallow. I thought he was clever, gifted. But he wasn't, no more than an animal. Did you ever own a dog, Ganley?"

"Just at the moment, I can't remember."

The lighter twirled in his hand and I froze with fear.

"Don't get funny. I had a dog, as a child. I mean a real dog, a wonderful dog called Bob. That's very symmetrical, isn't it? The two Bobs."

"Did you kill him in the car, like this?"

Pelling's mind came back on lazy flapping wings. He was sitting there drenched in petrol, thinking about his first chum called Bob and all the sticks he had retrieved, all the biscuits he had balanced on the end of his nose. He studied me with a faint frown.

"No. No, not in the car. We drove to Angoulême and met him off the train. I wanted to see his face when he realised that Melissa was with me. It was worth seeing. He had a fraction of a second to decide what to do. And he smiled and kissed her. Then he turned and hugged me. He was afraid, all right, but he overcame it. He calculated what he could get away with, what he needed to do to get us out of the station and into the car. That was his method, you know, with women: one step at a time, one little victory followed by another. At least have a drink, at least let's talk about it. He told me all that. More than once he told me all that."

"Listen, Pelling. I want you to give me the lighter."

"Oh no. I haven't finished."

"No, but you can finish outside, over there. See the little piece of grass in the sunlight? We can sit down and—"

He waved the thing in front of my face. His thumb was on the wheel.

"I told you about the farmhouse where I first met him. I told you about that. I asked him then, that very first time, whether all that he was telling me – the victories, his conquests – weren't another way of saying he hated women. No, he said. It's just that I'm not afraid of them."

"And you thought that was a hell of a deep remark."

"Yes," Pelling said simply. "At the time I did."

"So, just to hurry the story along a bit—"

"Shut up!" Pelling shouted at the top of his voice. "Shut your filthy mouth! You show me some respect, Ganley. You *listen* to me. Somebody is going to listen to me before I die. Even somebody as disgusting as you."

"Go ahead."

But instead he brooded for a full minute. The petrol sloshing round our feet was vaporising all the time – though I parked in what I hoped was shade, the sun was bursting over the windscreen. Sweat trickled round my ribs.

"The girl in Tangier was a demonstration of his way with women. We nearly killed her. We paid her a lot of money and then went on well past the moment that money could mean anything. I was afraid, of course. I was terrified. He did most of it, but I was there, I saw how she fought. I took it for granted she would go to the police. She didn't. She lay on the bed with all this money scattered over her, stuffed between her legs, looking at us with utter loathing – and nothing happened. In the morning she was gone. He had proved a point."

"And then the same thing happened to Melissa."

"Yes," Pelling said absently. His mind was far, far way. He rubbed his thumb lightly over the flint wheel, making a scratching noise that sounded like thunder.

"Killing him was going to be a way of killing something in

231

myself. That was the plan. It was a way of taking myself out of that Tangier bedroom, with the girl tied to the bed by her tights. I was being driven by him, like a farmer driving a beast. I thought I could stop it. I had to stop it."

"Never mind the girl in Tangier."

He looked at me with an expression of curiosity.

"I'm telling you why I killed him."

"To purify yourself."

"Yes."

"Good. Now, I'm going to open the door and get out, Pelling. You want to blow yourself up, go ahead. But I'm just that bit fussy about who I'm seen dead with."

And I turned as if to open the door, swung round with my left arm stiffened and locked at the elbow, and smashed him in the windpipe. Then I opened the door. Then – but only after picking myself up off the road ten metres away, still whole, still alive – I walked round to the passenger door, got him out and dragged him into the woods. His hat fell off, his glasses tumbled. One shoe was left behind, snagged on a root. I searched him for the lighter and then threw myself down beside him, loving grass and leaves and ants with a sobbing fervour I had not found in myself since childhood.

"You brought him straight from Angoulême?"

"We took him back to the house and gave him a meal. Not a meal, a snack. Something to drink. That was partly what he wanted. Time, of course, to work out the angles. And our acquiescence, that everything was in the end ordinary – small talk, flushing lavatories, cigarettes and coffee. And duty free scotch. Little pebbles to build a cairn. He was a genius at deflecting hate."

"And then something very unexpected happened," I said slowly.

232

Naked, he was absurdly thin. His knees were like clubs. His pale skin was stretched over his bones like parchment. I had made him take off his sodden clothes and pile them in the shade. We could see the road and the car but were partially screened by bushes. Pelling sat with his knees up, his arms hugging his shins.

"I can't tell you that."

"Then let me tell *you*. Pilar turned up."

"No, of course not."

"I think she did. Because otherwise how would Melissa have thought she might have done it? You were wondering what the hell to do, and she pitched up. She'd followed you down. Look at me, Tony."

"Yes," he said, after a long pause.

"And you were surprised?"

"I was maddened by it."

"She didn't trust you to handle it alone."

Without his glasses, Pelling's eyes were weak and defenceless. He pulled a fallen branch towards him and began peeling the bark with his thumbnails, scattering white grubs and ants onto his shins.

"I worshipped her. That was almost literally true. She was everything I ever wanted. I'd looked for her all my life. You wouldn't understand that. And Westerman sat there watching, thinking it was going to be all right. He began to preen himself, even. It was still very awkward, anything could happen – but he could see a chink of light. He could see a way of playing us all off against one another."

"How would he do that?"

Pelling smiled sadly.

"I began to see that if I let him sleep there, if he could go to sleep with Pilar and Melissa in the same house, if the four of us just gave up and slept, he would have won. Not won – he

would have got away with it, what he's done to Melissa…
And that's what he was edging towards – that we should all
get drunk and then the worst moment would pass."

He passed a hand over his face, thinking about it, and
rapped the branch on the ground to shake off the insects. His
fingernails were filled with moss and black bark. He smelt
them experimentally.

"Pilar took Melissa to a hotel. There is one, not a very
good one, about six kilometres away. It was one in the morning. The moon was full. We were sitting out in the yard, shouting, drinking. When I looked round the women had gone. And
Westerman was relaxed now. He was very relaxed. I
suggested we go for a drive."

"Why?"

"That was his question. He was laughing at me."

"Had you talked about Melissa?"

"He did the talking. He told me things about Pilar, about
her real background. He was saying to me: look, this is what
you are. You have a daughter, and a whore for a housekeeper.
And me for a friend. You are a certain person. A certain kind
of person. And there's nothing you can do about it. So I kept
suggesting we go for a drive."

He stared at me, as if surprised to find me still there, still
listening. And I thought of him sleeping in her bedroom in his
big house and the secrets of the first floor that the cleaning
lady had to be prevented from seeing. I thought of him standing at the door of the room he had made for Pilar, looking at it
all in bemusement.

"Westerman was the Devil, do you see? He was something
you have to force out of yourself. The Devil lives in everybody.
In most people he only goes there to sleep. They sense him, but
they never meet him face to face. I was unlucky."

"What made him go with you?"

234

"Happiness," Pelling said, staring.

And I could picture them, drunk, trying to reverse the car out of the courtyard, driving away into the powdery moonlight, raping the calm and the silence.

"How did you kill him?"

"With a hammer. It's here somewhere. I threw it away. I drove him back into Angoulême and threw him over the ramparts. It was quite easy. There were no problems. Once he was dead, he was nothing. I had washed my hands of him."

He stood, dragging himself up by the branch he had skinned.

"I would like to get some clean clothes from the boot of my car."

"I'll do it."

"I'm not going anywhere, Ganley."

"All the same—" I began.

The branch hit me across the bridge of the nose and I fell back. Pelling's bony nakedness skipped to the road, and when I struggled up he was inside and turning the ignition. The car started first time as good cars do, and he drove away. He crossed the lowest part of the ravine, started up the other side and met, coming down, a tractor and trailer in the very centre of the road.

Some of the debris showered down through the trees where I was standing and watching. The little wood hissed with flying metal. Gobs of yellow flame hung whimsically in the branches before falling to the ground. Of the largest shadows in the sky thrown up out of the fireball, one was the bonnet of the car. I fell to my knees like a believer; and like a believer, I spoke directly to God.

NINETEEN

I went to say goodbye to Pilar two days later. She lay on a while melamine beach lounger in the garden of M. Delcasse, her ribs strapped, with a black eye and a splinted finger as additional trophies. I kissed her on her cheek and sat down beside her. Her hair was scraped back and tied in a little red bow, making her look wide awake and faintly astonished.

"Good digs? Food okay?"

"You look worse than *I* do," she said. "Have you been sleeping in the street?"

"More or less. How are you getting on with Delcasse?"

"You should let him give you some of his old clothes, Ganley. I'm sure he would."

"Are you going to be okay?"

"It's perfect here. Denzil is jealous as all fall down, and he hasn't even met Roberto yet – the Italian boyfriend. Who's a dish. Twenty two and looks every inch of it. Of course I'm going to be okay. I'm in safe hands, as they say."

We sat watching the martins swoop this way and that over the roof of the church. M. Delcasse's palm tree swayed languorously above geometrically perfect rakings of gravel.

236

Inside the house, the owner pecked at a typewriter. The noise was somehow very comforting.

"I came to say goodbye."

"That was nice of you. I won't say keep in touch, because unless I'm very unlucky I won't see or hear from you again."

"That's the way it goes, Pilar."

"Yes," she said. "If you do it properly, that's the way it goes. What's happening with Diane and Melissa?"

I hesitated. Pilar smiled and offered me her tiny little hand. I brought it to my lips and kissed it.

"Come on," she said. "Be sensible. You're always going to lose that one."

"You take care of yourself, you hear?"

"I can do that."

We stared at each other a long moment while Delcasse's typewriter picked up speed, as though he had just hit on a really good bit his fingers could not wait to transpose. Then I bent and kissed her on the cheek.

Denzil was in the square in front of the church, playing football with the village kids. A group of four old men sat on a rusty iron bench, their sticks between their legs. They managed to convey a disdain, a peasant indifference that reached back all the way to the days when the English army swaggered through here on their way back from the ruinous battle of Poitiers, kicking up dust in just the same way. Denzil darted to intercept a soft lob, took it on his chest, thence to his feet, back to knee, up to his head and then kicked the ball high into the air. It hung against the cloudless blue, seeming for a magic moment that it might stay there forever. I turned away and walked to the car, pretending that the shouts were of joy at something never seen before on earth.

Wanting that to happen – waiting for it – is no way to live your life. Ask anybody.

237

Brian Thompson was born in Lambeth, London, and after the usual adventures read English at Cambridge. For thirteen years he taught at various levels of secondary and higher education, without ever getting the hang of it. In 1973 he began writing for a living, which is merely to indicate credits in television and radio drama too numerous and too ephemeral to list. Of his eight stage plays, the best known are *Tishoo* and *Turning Over*. He has published four novels. His biography of the nineteenth century eccentric Mrs Georgina Weldon is published later this year as *A Monkey among the Crocodiles*. He spends his time now between Oxford and la France profonde.

For further information about Slow Dancer Press
visit our web site
www.mellotone.co.uk
or join our free mailing list.
For further information about Slow Dancer Press
visit our web site
www.mellotone.co.uk
or join our free mailing list.

Slow Dancer Press
91 Yerbury Road London N19 4RW
slowdancer@mellotone.co.uk